The Footsteps Were Real. . . . And They Were Coming Nearer!

"Didn't you hear it?" Maury whispered.

"What?"

"Listen!"

Then . . . from a distance, a slight shuffling sound. Maury didn't move.

Chip held his breath, straining to hear. Yes . . . there was a sound . . . a slight sound . . . on the stairway.

The shuffling continued, step by step, louder now, and closer.

Then there was silence, more frightening than sound. It was as though the house and everyone in it was holding its breath. Chip's body felt like one big, fast heartbeat. *There was something on the landing. Waiting . . .*

Books by Stella Pevsner

AND YOU GIVE ME A PAIN, ELAINE
CALL ME HELLER, THAT'S MY NAME
CUTE IS A FOUR-LETTER WORD
FOOTSTEPS ON THE STAIRS
I'LL ALWAYS REMEMBER YOU . . . MAYBE

Available from ARCHWAY paperbacks

Footsteps
On The Stairs

Stella Pevsner

Illustrated by Barbara Seuling

AN ARCHWAY PAPERBACK
Published by POCKET BOOKS • NEW YORK

An Archway Paperback published by
POCKET BOOKS, a division of Simon & Schuster, Inc.
1230 Avenue of the Americas, New York, N.Y. 10020

ISBN: 0-671-52411-9

First Archway Paperback printing July, 1984

10 9 8 7 6 5 4 3

AN ARCHWAY PAPERBACK and colophon are
trademarks of Simon & Schuster, Inc.

Printed in the U.S.A.

IL 3+

For Charlie

Contents

1

An ESP Trial Run

CHIP SANDERS sat at the desk in his room and pressed his fingers against the mast of his ship. The model he had just glued together looked pretty tacky compared with the painting on the lid of the box. The picture showed full sails blowing in the wind, blue waves, clouds, and even seagulls.

The plastic model was gray. There were no sails, and wouldn't be unless Chip could talk his sister Fran into making some, which was unlikely. The mast needed more glue, but there wasn't any left.

I'm scuttled, Chip thought, liking the sound of the words. Scuttled, sunk. The ship had wiped out his savings, and allowance day was a week off.

Maybe he could borrow some kind of glue from Fran. She was always involved in an art project. Right now, in fact, she was downstairs with her friends Debbie and Veronica making something. He might as well use the glue as an excuse and go down to investigate.

In the kitchen, the phone rang. "Chip, it's for you," his mother called.

When Chip picked up the receiver and heard a sneeze, he knew it was his friend Arnold. Arnold was allergic to almost everything, including the telephone.

"I thought," Chip said, "you were going to come over."

"I had to go to the Park District with my dad," Arnold said, "to sign up for swim lessons. You going to . . .?"

"Are you kidding? I hate swimming. Besides, it's too cold in October."

"What's the difference? The pool's indoors. Well, so long."

"So long. You want to come over now?"

"Okay." They hung up.

When Chip got back to his room, the mast was listing to starboard. Sighing, he straightened it and held it in place, hoping the glue would set.

From the register near his feet sounds filtered from the basement. Chip heard the murmur of Fran's voice. Then the words of Debbie the Drip came through loud and clear . . . "Not that way . . . you'll spoil it!" Boy, was she bossy! He didn't see how his sister could stand her for a friend. His eyes rested on the painting of his ship, and he thought with satisfaction of Debbie walking the plank. She'd probably still be yakking as she struck water.

Veronica, now, was different. She didn't act like a Big Wheel just because she was a teenager. She still talked to Chip and once in a while even climbed trees or rode a bicycle. And she didn't carry on about clothes and makeup, even though she had once lived in Hollywood.

Chip didn't hear the doorbell, but suddenly he knew Arnold was coming down the hall because of the series of sneezes.

"Hey, take it easy," Chip said, as Arnold paused at the door, all stiffened up. "You may blast my ship to smithereens."

Arnold trapped a mighty sneeze in the bottom of his sweatshirt. "Whew, that one really cleared my sinuses," he said. "I sure am allergic to something in this house."

Arnold had light, wispy hair and rather large front teeth. He looked delicate and younger than his ten years. Until he started speaking. His voice was surprisingly deep. "Still on the ship jag," he now observed.

Chip's fingers felt stiff and uncomfortable. "Any reason why I shouldn't be?" he asked a bit irritably.

"I've been wondering if you were a sailor in your preexistence," Arnold said, brushing aside an empty box and settling into the easy chair. "You seem obsessed with the sea."

"I just like ships," Chip said. "What do you mean, *preexistence?*"

"Your former life. Whoever you were before you were born as Chip Sanders. It so happens

3

that I saw a demonstration on TV last night. They hypnotized this guy and took him 'way back. It was fascinating. I thought of calling you, but it was so late I knew your parents would get mad."

"How do they do it? Take someone 'way back?"

"I just told you. Under hypnosis. It's pretty creepy. This guy began talking about the Civil War. He must have been a Rebel because he had a Southern accent."

"No kidding!" Chip carefully let go of the mast. It held. "I'd like to be hypnotized some day."

"So would I. But my scientific objectivity might stand in the way. I may be too strong willed."

"Yeah," Chip said. "Hey, Arnold, did you bring the new set of cards?"

"Sure did. I'll set them up."

They arranged five stacks of cards on the floor. Each top card had a symbol—a red circle, a purple square, a yellow triangle, an orange X, and a green star.

"There are five of each, like before," Arnold said. "I used stiffer cardboard this time, so there won't be so much chance of the cards bending and giving us some kind of clue. You want to go first?"

"Okay." Chip opened up a loose-leaf notebook labeled PRIVATE—ESP. "At last count, I was slightly ahead of you in performance."

"My strong will, again, getting in the way,"

Arnold said, sitting cross-legged on the floor. "Let's review the scores. It may give me some incentive."

Chip turned back the pages. "On September twentieth, we made ten runs each . . . that means each of us tried to guess the twenty-five symbols ten different times."

"Oh, come on. I know that. Just give me the scores."

"I averaged out five hits in each run. You guessed around three out of each twenty-five."

"I don't think I was feeling so well that day," Arnold observed.

Chip turned to the next page. "You went up to four, the next time, and I dropped to about four and a half." He studied the next page. "Then we both dropped to three."

"Some people have to build up their powers," Arnold said. "ESP isn't something that just strikes like lightning."

"Shall I go on?" Chip asked, turning more pages.

"Naw. Let's get on with today's experiment. Although don't be surprised if I'm not up to par, after last night." He scooped up the cards and shuffled them. "Is your mind clear?"

Chip put his hands over his eyes and breathed deeply while Arnold sat waiting. "Okay. Ready."

Arnold put a card face down on the floor.

"Triangle," Chip said.

Arnold turned it over. Square. He laid down the next card.

"Star."

"Nope."

After five tries, Chip guessed correctly. Arnold set that card aside.

"Square," Chip said next. Correct.

When Arnold had laid down the final card, there were eight correct guesses.

"Wow!" Chip felt a surge of power. "I'm really with it today."

"Do me now," Arnold said.

Chip recorded his score and shuffled the cards.

"Circle," Arnold called out for the first card.

"Correct."

"Square." A miss.

"Circle again." Wrong.

He continued to miss. A peal of laughter drifted through the register.

"I can't concentrate with all that racket," Arnold complained. "What are they doing downstairs anyway?"

"Let's go and find out."

"Will they let you?"

"It's my basement, too," Chip pointed out, scooping up the cards. "Let's just write on the page for today *'Experiment Discontinued, Conditions Unsatisfactory.'* "

"Suits me."

Chip lettered the words, and then pausing at his eight score, gave it an asterisk. "Just to remind me to try to equal it next time," he explained.

The basement, which even on good days was

a place Mrs. Sanders would never let any of her friends see, was in a worse clutter than usual. The girls had covered the Ping-Pong table with an old plastic tablecloth. It was heaped with orange and black scraps of paper, cans of paint, and an old net curtain that looked as though it had been dragged through a trash heap.

Fran and Debbie were bending over a big piece of poster board, pasting on a horrible witch mask.

"Neat!" Chip exclaimed, leaning on the table to get a better look. "What's that for?"

Fran frowned. "Chip, you're jiggling. What do you want?"

"Some glue," he said, remembering his ship.

"You can't use ours," Debbie said. "We need it. So why don't you two buzz off?"

"It's my basement, don't forget," Chip said. "I have a right to be here."

"Honey," Fran said in a voice which resembled her mother's when she had a headache and wanted to avoid a scene, "why don't you run along? We're making a poster for the Fun Fair at school, and you're supposed to be surprised."

"Well, I'm not going to be," Chip said stubbornly.

Veronica came from the laundry room with a brush and a can of water. "Hi, boys," she said. "Come to give us ideas for the Spook House?"

"Spook House!" Chip exclaimed. "You in charge of it this year?"

"I sure am," Veronica said, making a monster face, "and I'm open to suggestions if you have any."

"Oh, honestly," Debbie said, giving Veronica a disgusted look. "If you're going to drag in the juveniles!" She wiped her hands on an old rag, and with just the tips of her fingers tilted the globe watch suspended on a chain around her neck. "I've got to run!" she squealed in her fakey grown-up voice. "My art class begins in thirty minutes. My mother will have fits! She's probably in the car right now, waiting."

In a soft voice, Chip said to Arnold, "Why doesn't witch-girl just fly to art class on her broom?"

"That's okay, Debbie," Veronica said. "We'll finish up here. Just tell us what to do."

With an important air, Debbie explained how they should dip the old gray netting into the paste mixture she had prepared, squeeze out the excess liquid, and drape the material onto the board so that the witch's face seemed to be peering out. "It will create quite an eerie effect, if done properly," she said. "And when it's finished, do the lettering. Give time, place, and so forth so the little kiddies at school will know where to go to get good and scared." She gave the briefest glance at Chip before turning back to the girls. "Au revoir, mesdemoiselles."

"Oh, reservoir," Veronica replied with a grin. She gave a sticky wave of her fingers to the departing Debbie. "I'm sure glad she's taking that course," she remarked to Fran. "Although I've got some pretty gory ideas for the Spook House, I'm just nowhere when it comes to pure art."

"Debbie's always taking courses," Fran said, dipping the net into the glue. "Did you know she's studied voice—and ballet?"

"Nope. Here, let me help you squeeze that out."

"And she took private tennis lessons last summer. Oh, well, you remember that. It's when we were swimming."

"She never swims, does she?" Veronica said, laying out the net at the top of the board while Fran held the soggy bulk at the bottom.

"No, she's afraid of getting her hair wet."

Chip snorted. "I'll bet she's afraid, period."

Fran turned to look at her brother. "I notice you steer clear of the pool yourself. You must be afraid, too."

"Ha. For your information, Arnold and I are taking swim lessons at the Park District. Starting next . . . starting soon. . . ." His voice trailed away as he realized what he had just said.

"I didn't know that," Fran said. "I take it back, then."

I wish I could, Chip thought. But he had committed himself before three people.

"Glad you changed your mind," Arnold said. "What made you do it?"

Chip smiled weakly and shrugged.

Arnold narrowed his eyes and appeared deep in thought, like when he was getting ready for an ESP run. Then he snapped his fingers. "I've got it!" he said. "It's probably your preexistence taking hold. Remember, I guessed you were a sailor at one time?"

Chip nodded. It was true enough that he was fascinated by ships. But even if Arnold was right, and he had once been a sea captain, that didn't mean a thing. He had been *on* the water, not *in* it.

"I have to confess," Arnold said, as they started back upstairs, "that the thought has entered my mind that you might be afraid. I should have known that you don't admit to fear in any form." ∙

"That's right," Chip mumbled. And it was right, in a way. He didn't admit it. But it was there. That deathly fear of water.

2

The House down the Street

THE TROUBLE with a teen-aged sister, Chip thought at dinner that night, was that as soon as you counted on her paying no attention, she zeroed in on you. "Look at his hands, Mother! They're grubby!" she'd sometimes shriek in the middle of one of her *Am I too short? Am I too fat?* kinds of conversations.

Now, hoping she'd keep up her usual chatter, Chip ate quietly, wondering how he might possibly squirm out of that statement he had made this afternoon. Arnold would understand if he backed out of swimming class and Veronica never interfered. If he could just get to Fran . . .

". . . because the basketball games will be Friday nights, too, right after school," she was saying.

"Absolutely not," Mr. Sanders said. "You're still too young to be at large that long. You just get yourself home for dinner and then take off for swimming."

"Speaking of swimming"—Fran's eyes turned toward Chip, and he knew this was it—"isn't it nice my brother finally decided to sign up? For lessons?"

"Who?" Mr. and Mrs. Sanders chorused, as though the house were crawling with brothers. *"Chip?"*

He felt himself blushing. "I just kind of said I might."

"You said you *were*," Fran reminded.

"Chip, that's wonderful," Mrs. Sanders said. "For you to decide all on your own. I always hoped you would."

"When are the lessons?" Mr. Sanders asked.

"I'm not sure. Maybe the classes are all filled up."

"If they're that popular we'd better get over Monday night to sign you up," Mr. Sanders said.

Chip sighed. Scuttled again.

The next day, Sunday, Chip and Fran went with their parents to visit Great-Aunt Clara and Aunt Margaret. Aunt Margaret, who was really their mother's cousin, was an art teacher. Right now, Fran was upstairs with the aunt-cousin working on a charcoal drawing, and Chip was sitting with the rest of the grown-ups, feeling miserable.

"Chip," his great-aunt suddenly remarked, "why aren't you helping yourself to these cookies? Don't you feel well?"

"I feel sort of weak, inside," he said. Then to give it a little more punch, added, "I have no energy."

Great-Aunt Clara looked concerned. "Helen, has he had a checkup lately? You never know . . ."

"He had a physical before school started. There's nothing wrong with him except lack of—"

"I don't read that late," Chip interrupted, knowing what she was about to say. "My light is off at nine thirty, like you insist."

"But, Chip, it's the *kind* of thing you read." To her aunt, Mrs. Sanders explained, "He's obsessed with books on the occult. Reading about ghosts just before closing his eyes . . . it's no wonder he moans in his sleep."

"Do I?" Chip asked. "Do I ever walk in my sleep?"

"No, and you'd better not start."

"Well, Chip," Great-Aunt Clara said, "I guess you live in the wrong neighborhood. Around here, we have the real thing."

"What thing?" Chip asked excitedly, forgetting he was supposed to be listless. "You mean there's a ghost? Where?"

Aunt Clara shook her head disapprovingly. "Supposedly in the Gaynor house. They say— oh, it's too foolish . . ."

"Right." Mr. Sanders clapped his hands on his knees. "I think I'll go fix that loose storm window, Clara. And, Chip, how about raking some leaves for your aunt? A little fresh air would do you good." He smiled. "And build up that resistance of yours."

"Okay. But, Dad, let me hear the end of this story. Else I'll keep wondering and never get to sleep tonight."

Chip's parents exchanged resigned looks. "The rake's in the garage," Mr. Sanders said. "And we're going to leave in about an hour."

Chip nodded and turned to his aunt. "Where's the Gaynor house?"

"Just down the street. That gray house on the corner. With all the bushes around it. It looks spooky all right, and I suppose that just adds to the tales."

"Who lives there? I never did meet anyone in all the years I've been coming here."

"That's because, after his wife died so suddenly, Mr. Gaynor always rented it to couples with no children. He was fussy about that house, having built it. But finally, I guess he got too old to look after it, because now it's been sold. And the stories have started up again."

"What stories?"

"Oh, Helen, he might as well know," Aunt Clara said, as Mrs. Sanders shifted suddenly in her chair, "then he'll see what nonsense it is." To Chip, she said, "According to some people, there are sounds in the house at night."

Mrs. Sanders picked up a magazine. "All houses have sounds in the night."

"But not . . . footsteps."

"Footsteps!" Chip felt his heart pounding.

15

"Footsteps in the house and up the stairs. That's what they say. And I don't believe a word of it."

If she doesn't believe a word of it, why did she lower her voice, Chip wondered.

"Have you ever been in the house?"

Aunt Clara snorted. "No, and I don't intend to. I don't believe any of that, mind you. But there must be something odd going on in that place."

"Chip," Mrs. Sanders said, closing the magazine, "you've heard the story. Now, please do as your father . . ."

"Right down the block . . ." Chip murmured, getting to his feet.

"No, right in the front yard. The leaves," his mother said firmly.

"Oh . . . kay."

Gee whiz. Work, work, work, he thought, dragging the rake and basket from the garage to the front yard. It's no wonder he was so run down. When he fell flat from exhaustion and had to be hauled off in an ambulance they'd all stand around him in the hospital sobbing, and blaming themselves. And when even the greatest medical brains of the world failed to save him, his folks would be haunted . . . haunted. He looked in the direction of the Gaynor place, but the house next door cut off his view.

To be stuck with leaves at a time like this! Just when he finally got the scent of a real-live supernatural manifestation. But there was no use howling about it.

16

He began raking furiously. As soon as he finished, he'd stroll down the street. He'd walk in front of the house, then turn the corner and eye it from the side. Then he'd circle back, cross the street, and take a stand. He wished there was a bus stop, so he wouldn't look so obvious. He could pretend to tie his shoe, and glance up from a squatting position. Then he could pretend to drop something and act like he was searching for it.

"Hi!"

The rake dropped from Chip's hands as he spun around.

It was only a boy about his own size.

"Oh, hi," Chip said. He started zipping his jacket, slowly, as though that was the reason he had dropped the rake. He glanced at the boy to see if he was laughing, but he just stood with his hands in his pockets, smiling in a friendly way.

"You live around here?" Chip asked. He had never seen the boy before.

"Yeah. Want me to help you with those leaves?"

"Sure, if you want to."

"I'm glad there's another kid in the neighborhood. I thought there were just girls." The boy scooped up an armful of leaves. "What's your name?"

"Chip Sanders. Only I don't live here. I'm visiting."

"Just my luck. This sure is a lonesome neighborhood."

17

If the kid only knew how lucky he was to live around here! Chip had an inspiration. He could pull this boy into the investigation. They could work as a team, and when he wasn't there, the boy could do some scouting around, ask a few discreet questions, and take notes. "You interested in psychic phenomena?" he asked as a starter.

"I might be," the boy said with a grin, "if I knew what it was."

"The supernatural. Spooks. Things that go bump in the night."

Was that fear in the boy's eyes? He began shaking his head and smiling. "There's no such thing," he said. "It's all in the mind."

"I guess so." Chip wasn't about to try to convince a skeptic. He'd just be friendly with this kid and go quietly on his investigation alone. "What's your name?"

"Maury. Maurice, really. Maury Kinkade. I'm ten and three-quarters, birthday's in January. Are you going Trick or Treating next week?"

Chip had almost forgotten about Halloween. "I guess I will," he said. "Always do. Because of the loot only, of course."

"What other reason would there be?"

Chip found it hard to explain. When he was little, he'd always been excited by witches, ghosts, and goblins roaming the streets. Now, the trend seemed to be for kids to be clowns, rag dolls or other sickening stuff. "I like the spooky side of Halloween," he said. "But there isn't much of that any more."

"In the town I came from, we used to have a Halloween Carnival," Maury said, picking up a rock from the grass and pitching it to the street. "There were games for the little kids and a costume dance for the grown-ups."

"What about the in-between guys?"

"They had carnival booths where you try for prizes, and a Spook House that was really something. I wish I could go back for it this year, but it's too far away of course."

Chip didn't understand this boy. A minute ago he'd acted as though he didn't care for the supernatural, and here he was, raving about a Spook House. Still, it wasn't really the same thing. "There's going to be a Spook House at the junior high in my neighborhood, if you're all that interested," he said.

"There is? Are you going?"

"Sure. You can come along if you want to."

"Thanks!" Maury's face glowed.

They kept raking and stomping down the leaves in the basket. The boy seemed so happy at finding a part-time friend that Chip abandoned his idea of shaking him as soon as they were finished. He'd just put off casing the Gaynor house until the next time he came to Aunt Clara's.

"You like sports?" Chip asked.

"Sure."

"Hockey?"

"You said it!"

They talked of the Stanley Cup Play-offs and the teams most likely to qualify in the coming season, as they worked.

After they had finally finished and carried the things to the back, Maury said, "I guess I ought to go home, now. I'll see you at the Fun Fair if it's okay with my folks."

"Sure. I'll walk you part way. Then I'll have to scram because it's about time for us to leave, too."

They moved in the direction of the Gaynor place. Chip listened to more of Maury's talk of hockey, but part of his attention was focused on the house ahead of them.

". . . so I guess my favorite team—what's the matter?" Maury asked.

Chip had stopped stock-still. The window at the back of the second floor . . . was it the dull afternoon light playing tricks or had there been a face—a ghostly face—leering down at them? "That window . . ." he pointed.

"My room. How did you guess? Hey, there's my mother, looking for me." He waved to a woman at the front door and darted in the direction of the house. "See you," he called back to Chip.

Chip's mouth moved, but he made no sound. In a moment Maury disappeared. Swallowed up by the grim, gray Gaynor house.

With a shiver, Chip turned and headed back for Great-Aunt Clara's.

3

The Halloween Wrap-up

How COULD he have been so dumb? Chip wondered as he jogged down the street. Not even guessing where Maury lived. It was so obvious. There were hardly ever any vacant houses in this old neighborhood. But he just hadn't connected the wholesome-looking boy with that sinister old place.

He was still thinking of it on the drive home. And then a zoom-bam thought struck. Here was the perfect setup! With a friend living in the house he'd have every reason to go inside and explore from top to bottom. Spook Houses, *yccck!* Here was the real thing, right in his lap, and he was going to make the most of it. But for the time being he'd keep that idea to himself, his parents feeling as they did about his interest in the occult.

He might confide in Arnold, though, and get the benefit of his keen, analytical mind. Fran, of course, was out. She'd rush right off to tell

Debbie, Miss Blabsville of Junior High. And everyone would laugh.

Spirits were nothing to laugh about. They could take revenge. Into your room at night, they could come, and . . . He gave an involuntary shiver.

"What's the matter?" Fran asked softly.

"Just thinking . . . about spooks," he murmured.

Her eyes widened. "You really must have ESP," she said. "I was just thinking of the Spook House."

"No kidding! What about it?"

"Some of the ideas we're dreaming up. It's going to be good and gory."

Chip smiled with satisfaction. Then Maury would get a lot out of it and their friendship would be off to a good start. But why would a boy who lived in a for-sure haunted house get a buzz from a fakey Spook House?

The week started off in a grim way, with Mr. Sanders trotting Chip right over, Monday night, to sign up for swim classes.

"Sure, I can fit you into the group Tuesdays and Thursdays," the man at the registry desk said. "There hasn't been a rush for enrollment this year."

"I wonder why," Chip said innocently.

"I don't know. The lads seem to get a lot out of it."

Like chlorine poisoning, pneumonia, and athlete's foot, Chip thought.

He made it a practice not to dwell upon unpleasant subjects. Time enough to think of them when they happened. Instead, he thought about his Trick or Treat costume for the coming Saturday.

Chip rejected his mother's suggestions, all of them simple to put together, like a hobo or an old lady with a shopping bag and sneakers. Finally, Thursday night Mrs. Sanders said, "Just don't surprise me like last year, when you decided the day of the event to be Sir Lancelot. I still haven't recovered."

"Okay. I guess I'll be a mummy."

"Mummy! Oh, Chip!"

"That's not so hard to do. All I need is an old sheet to tear into strips."

"But it's so . . . grim. All right, go ahead, but you're on your own. Now, how about you two clearing up the dishes?"

Chip put the dishes on the counter dividing the dining room the kitchen. Fran lifted them to the sink. Their house, a typical one in the newer section of town, was built for saving steps. Chip had always thought it an okay place to live, but now he could see it was pretty dull. Not like Maury's, with those two stories and a creaking staircase and probably all kinds of cool out-of-the-way closets and corners and hiding places. He could hardly wait to get inside and explore. But first he had to follow through on his promise to Maury to meet him at the Fun Fair. He'd call when no one was around and set it up.

"Come on, Chip, stop daydreaming," Fran said, waiting for more dishes. "Your mummy idea isn't bad. How are you going to get around, though, in a case?"

"You know I can't be in a case. I have to stay loose. It's not important to look all that authentic anyway, for Trick or Treating. Most people just drop a candy bar into your sack and bam, slam the door. Unless you're little and cute."

"Still . . . for the Spook House." Fran turned, dripping water onto the floor. "If you'd be willing to be strapped to an ironing board, or better yet, one of those reclining things like Debbie's mother has, maybe you could help haunt the place. Should I speak to Veronica about it?"

Chip felt a rush of excitement. Any other year he'd have leaped at the chance. But now he had a more important mission than scaring a bunch of kids at a Fun Fair. He was onto the real thing. And he had a commitment to Maury.

"Thanks, Fran, but I guess not," he said. "I wouldn't want to butt in on you girls."

Fran looked at him skeptically, but said nothing.

The mummy costume proved a mistake. First, Arnold wrapped Chip's legs so tightly in the strips of sheet, he couldn't bend them. When he loosened the bandages, the rows slipped up and down. Pieces of adhesive tape helped hold the rows together, but spoiled the effect. Another thing. When Arnold did Chip's head, he had to leave the ears uncovered, not so much because of hearing, but so Chip would have something to hook his glasses onto. By the time Chip realized he couldn't get his wrapped feet into shoes and would have to slosh around in his winter boots, he was thoroughly disgusted.

"Come on, Arnold, let's get this rat race over with," he said, walking gingerly out of the room. His wrappings slipped with each step.

"You got the map?" Arnold asked, flicking the tassel of his graduation cap out of his eyes. His costume was a cinch. He had inherited some relative's paper cap and gown from June graduation. "I'm glad you had the foresight to make a map last year of the houses that gave the best treats. It will be a real time-saver."

"Yeah. Let's go."

"Sometimes your perception amazes me," Arnold added.

"Sometimes it amazes me, too," Chip said modestly, his good humor somewhat restored. "Now, we begin our route at the Wilmerts' and—" He stopped, stunned, his hand resting on his hip pocket.

"What's the matter? You look so funny."

"The map . . ." Chip stammered. "It's in my pocket. And I'm all wrapped up over it!"

By the next week, Chip was able to look back on Halloween night and smile. After a while, he had ripped away the strips of sheet and pulled out the map. People didn't seem to notice he was at loose ends. By cutting through to the best places he and Arnold had made a good haul. Next year, they'd start earlier and follow the same route. In the meantime, he had other things to think about.

So far, he hadn't said anything to Arnold about Maury. He didn't want Arnold zeroing in on the kid with questions or giving him that keen analytical look of his.

Chip started out easy when he called Maury after school on Wednesday. Information had the number.

"How are things?" Chip began.

"Fine."

"Still want to go to the Fun Fair?"

"Sure. It's nice of you to call, Chip. I was afraid you had forgotten."

Wow. How could he forget? "No, I really meant it. I'd like to see you again." And to explore your house, he thought. He was ashamed of thinking that. He'd hate to be the kind of guy who was nice to someone just for what he could get out of it. But he did like Maury. How could anyone help but like him?

"It's this Saturday, remember," Chip said. "Can you meet me around ten o'clock, at the door of the room that says FISHPOND?"

"Sure. What school?"

"Hillcrest. On Hillcrest Street."

"I'll find it. Thanks loads, Chip."

Hanging up, Chip wondered once again why

a boy who had said there were no such things as spooks was so interested in Spook Houses. But did he really not believe or was he just saying that? And how did he feel about living in a house where really truly strange things happened . . . or were said to happen? Chip would find out. And fast.

4

Haunting the Spook House

ON SATURDAY morning, the day of the Fun
Fair, Chip waited impatiently for Arnold. Mrs.
Sanders, slated for restaurant duty, had already gone. "I'll buy your lunch," she had
said, "if you'll shine around before one
o'clock."

Once again, Chip checked the time. Two
minutes to eleven! Maury would be wondering
what happened. Chip grabbed his jacket. He'd
go, and not even leave a note on the door.
"Englehardt," he'd say, "you're so hot on
ESP, didn't you get the thought message?"

As he reached the end of the driveway, Mrs.
Englehardt drove up with Arnold.

"I had to have my allergy shot," Arnold
explained, making room for Chip on the front
seat. "It's very painful." Before, he had always said it was like a mosquito bite. "I'd rest
awhile, but I know how anxious you are to get
to the Fun Fair," he said, with a glance at Chip
to see if he appreciated the sacrifice.

As soon as his mother zoomed off from the school grounds, Arnold headed for the pony rides. "It's best to go early before the animals get tired," he said. "You get a longer ride."

"Forget it," Chip said. "I'm late now, meeting Maury." He started away and Arnold followed. "Anyway, I thought you were allergic to horses."

"I get shots. Who's Maury?"

"A kid I know." Maybe Chip wouldn't bring Arnold into the Gaynor house investigation after all. It would serve him right for being such a goof-off.

Maury was waiting at the FISHPOND sign. His face broke into a broad smile at sight of Chip.

Chip introduced the boys. "Maury," he explained briefly to Arnold, "lives near my Aunt Clara. Shall we head for the Spook House?"

"What's the rush?" Arnold asked. "I'd like to try for a goldfish first."

"Aw, come on!" Chip exclaimed. "We're not interested—"

"Maybe you're not, you have a houseful of pets, but with my allergies, fish are about the only thing—"

"That's all right," Maury soothed. "There's time, isn't there?" It was hard to tell if he was being chicken or agreeable. "How do you win a fish anyway? There's such a crowd, you can't see inside."

"Simple," Chip said. "They're in little bowls and you throw Ping-Pong balls at them.

If one lands in the water you win the fish . . . bowl and all.''

"I'd like to try," Maury said. "If you don't mind." Kids were edging out of the room, some of them sloshing prizes around.

"Then let's buy some tickets and get in line."

It took a long time to get inside the room, and finally up to the rope. Arnold handed the father-in-charge his ticket and pitched three balls. The last hit a rim but glanced off. "Here's another ticket," Arnold said. "I'm warmed up now."

"Sorry, Sonny, you'll have to go to the end of the line."

Chip thought he might as well win a fish for Maury. He misjudged the weight of the Ping-Pong balls. Every one fell short.

Chip's cheeks felt warm. "I'm used to baseballs," he said loudly.

Maury made it on the last throw and landed a plump orange fish. He couldn't have looked happier.

"Nice going," Chip said. Pride forced him to get back in line. Arnold was already there. Maury edged along to keep them company. "You'll win this time," he encouraged. "Both of you."

Neither did.

"Let's try something else," Arnold suggested, "to change our luck."

In the dart game, Chip broke a balloon and won a nail puzzle.

31

They came to the Cake Walk. Although the game took forever, Arnold persuaded them to keep playing, until he finally won a chocolate two-layer.

Now, Chip was low on tickets. "We'd better head for the lunchroom," he said. "And then, off to the Spook House!"

The cafeteria was decorated in country style, with checked tablecloths and banners. Chip saw a couple of teachers, looking like any other parents, with their squirming little kids. He looked for his mother behind the serving counter.

"Hi, Chip," one of the women said. "Your mother left about ten minutes ago."

Aghast, Chip moved some streamers to look at the clock. Twenty after one. Oh, no, he'd have to pay for his own lunch!

Even though he skipped dessert, he had only two tickets left for the Spook House. The cause of his poverty was nonchalantly crunching ice from the bottom of his paper cup.

Chip pushed back his chair. "We're going upstairs, now," he said. "You coming, Arnold?"

"Later. I want to head back to the fishpond. Third time is charm, you know." He tilted his cup.

"One-track mind," Chip muttered as he and Maury went up the stairs. In the past he had often envied Arnold's concentration on the problem at hand. It was an asset in scientific investigations. But sometimes, like now, it was sickening.

The Spook House was off in a corridor by itself. The lighting was dim. Chip and Maury got at the end of the line. There weren't any little kids.

A sudden shrieking erupted from the exit door down the hall as people spilled from the room. A couple of junior high girls were hanging onto each other, giving little yells as they headed for the stairway.

"Next eight people," the girl at the entrance door said. "I'll count you off."

Chip's heart was pounding with anticipation. Would it really be good and gory? Maury was number seven and Chip eight. "That's all," the girl said. "Tickets, please."

The door closed behind them. It was pitch-black. Whisperings, giggles, and then silence as they waited. For what?

The darkness softened to reveal a black-robed figure with a mask. "You are to enter one by one," the figure intoned. It didn't sound like Veronica. "Hold onto the rope to guide you safely through the swamps of the spirits." Someone made a gulping noise. "Then tread through the maze—and don't falter—or you may become like one of the victims you will see on every side of you. Bewarrrrrrre . . . and take carrrrre. Prepare yourself for HORROR!"

The figure turned away and from the distance came sounds . . . a clanking of chains, a hollow beat . . . and then sounds like heavy breathing . . . and a *scream!*

Chip's group screamed, too. The curtains parted, letting in a faint, eerie light, and one person was pushed through as she begged, "Not me . . . not me . . . I don't want to be first!" She disappeared. They heard her scream.

Another went, and then another. Organ music boomed and subsided, and then more ghostly noises. "Neat," Maury whispered and disappeared beyond the curtain. Finally the robed figure pushed Chip forward.

He remembered to grab onto the rope. It was something to hang onto, and he needed something. To his right was a mass of tombstones, leaning this way and that, glowing with greenish lights. A mist rose from the ground and— yikes—something was rising in the air from behind . . . spooks! The noise in the background was a wailing, mournful sound. Chip felt his way along in the blackness, guided by the rope. The rope ended and he could barely make out irregular black walls. They turned, he could tell, because there were faint lights ahead.

He hurried forward toward the light and gasped.

There, in the bend of walls was a skeleton, holding a lantern. Chip had seen skeletons before, but this one shook him, the way it was leaning forward, leering. "Maury!" Chip

hissed. "Here . . . " came a whisper from ahead.

Chip moved on, then caught his breath. There was a ghastly scarred face with matted hair . . . and oh my gosh, eyeballs half out of the sockets. The bony hands seemed to move and Chip hurled himself forward.

The next grisly sight was a head. Just a head, on a board. Below the head was a bucket and something was drip, drip, dripping. Blood! As Chip lurched toward the exit, something hairy brushed his cheek. He whirled, to stare into the face of a monster ape . . . and it was alive! Its paw reached forward and opened the curtain. Chip flung himself through it and then through the exit door.

Maury, clutching his fishbowl, was standing in the hall. "Neat, eh?"

"Yeah, it was okay," Chip said. "I see Arnold isn't here, yet. Let's go through again and try to figure out how they did it." Maury nodded and they got back in line.

"Were you shook up?" Chip asked.

"Some. But I was glad to know it was all a fake."

"I wish I didn't know," Chip said. "It would be more fun."

"You wouldn't say that if . . . " Maury caught his lip in his teeth.

"If what?" Chip prodded.

There was a look of fright in Maury's eyes that instant before he lowered them. "Nothing."

He's really scared, Chip thought. Something has got to him. And it isn't the Spook House.

The second time through Chip happened to be last again. It was the same as before except for one thing. When the ape reached to open the curtain, it whispered, "Chip?"

"Huh?" He shrank back a little.

"It's me. Veronica. Listen, after this next bunch, we have to have intermission to fix things up. Stick around here at the door and I'll let you in. I have to ask you something."

"Sure," Chip whispered, excited. "Can I bring my friend Maury, too?"

"Yeh. Scram now, some more kids are coming."

While they were waiting, feeling excited, they spotted Arnold at the entrance door, toward the back of the line. He was holding a fishbowl in one hand and his cake box in the other.

"Don't let him see us," Chip said, pulling Maury against the wall, behind the last bunch of kids coming out. As Arnold, along with others, howled his disapproval over the announced delay, Chip and Maury slipped through the exit door and called to Veronica.

"Oh, hi," she said, poking her head through the curtain. She still had on the ape suit, but the head was missing. She flicked on lights in the Spook House. What a difference!

The "maze" was a bunch of screens, painted black. The head was made of a papier-mâché and the dripping blood was fake, of course. "I

37

made it myself," Veronica explained. "It's just food coloring, cornstarch, and water, brought to a boil." The lurching figure was stuffed clothes with a mask and fake rubber hands. The eyeballs were made of marbles pushed into boiled small potatoes. The skeleton was real, all right, borrowed from some medical lab.

"Where did you get your costume?" Chip asked Veronica.

"Oh, you know my Gramma Alice used to work in wardrobe out in Hollywood," she said, leading the boys beyond the screens. "She borrowed this for me, from *Planet of the Apes*. I love it. Follow me." She slipped under the rope into the "graveyard." The tombstones were cardboard. Behind them lay flattened piles of white cheesecloth. Ghosts. "Watch out for the wires," Veronica warned. Almost invisible nylon wires were attached to the spooks to make them rise on pulleys overhead. "They're all connected," Veronica explained. "Fran, over there in the corner, operates them all, like puppets."

One girl crawled on the floor, putting dry ice into bowls of water behind the tombstones. With each kerplunk, more mist arose. "The stuff wears out pretty fast," Veronica explained.

"How did you get the weird lights?" Maury asked. "That glow on things?"

"Black light. You paint everything with fluorescent paint, then when you turn on the black spotlight it picks up the paint and nothing else. It's an old technique. They use it a lot in plays for kids. Now, here's our problem." She stepped over a tombstone to the place where the curtain rounded. "Joyce, here, has to leave for her clarinet lesson. Do either of you guys know how to run a tape recorder?"

"Sure," the boys chorused.

"Okay, how about taking over? We're about ready to close up anyway. We're pooped."

"Hurry up," the girl at the door hissed. "They're getting mad out there in the hall."

"The tape is set with sounds. Turn them up or down or add your own noises. See you. Have to put on my head." She hurried off.

The boys examined the set. The mike flicked on with a switch. They sat cross-legged, half giggling, hardly able to believe their good luck.

"Hey, Maury," Chip whispered as the hall door opened to let the first eight victims into the now black room, "let's fix Arnold."

"How?"

"Really shake him up. For once, make him lose control. Help me watch for him."

Chip turned on the tape recorder and chuckled as sounds came out that had seemed so spooky before.

The first to enter was some boy who barged along. One girl, then, and another who shrieked and carried on like crazy. Chip turned the volume down and moaned . . . "Your timmmmme has commmmme!"

The group of eight went through, but no Arnold.

"He must have been too far back in line," Chip said. "Or else he turned chicken. Here comes the next batch."

They heard the girl at the door say, "All right, since this is everyone, we'll let all ten of you in." The hall door finally shut and the routine started again.

This time Maury worked the sound. Then he handed the mike to Chip, whispering, "Here comes Arnold."

Chip licked his lips. "Englehardt . . . " he moaned, "youuuu are marked!" There was a dark blob where Arnold's mouth had probably dropped open. Maury reached for the mike and murmured, "You dare to scoff at spirits. We will creep into your room tonight . . . and"—he thrust the mike at Chip—"and GRAB you!" Chip yelled. There was a clatter as someone stumbled, crashing Arnold into a screen.

"My fish!" he yelled.

Kids in the line laughed. "Throw him a hook!" someone called.

"Fishee . . . fishee . . ." Arnold's voice was muffled as he groped in the darkness. "Turn on the lights, you creeps! Someone may step on it!"

"Step on it!" a boy called. "Help stamp out sardines!"

"No lights, or our money back!" another boy shouted.

"Here it is," a girl called. "Take the slimy thing."

There was squealing as the fish passed from hand to hand and a slurp as it finally hit water.

"Move on!"

Chip whispered to Maury, "Let's see if he can get past the ape without sneezing. Or does he take shots for that, too?"

The group filed out, with just a scream or two from the girls.

"I have to hand it to Arnold," Chip admitted. "In spite of everything, he didn't lose control. All he lost was the fish."

"And just for a minute. You know, I ought to give him my fish, too. I forgot we have a new cat at home. He's awfully cute."

"I'd like to see him.

Someone turned on the lights.

Chip stretched. "Well, I guess that does it, for the Spook House. By Monday you'd never know it had been here."

"Wouldn't it be great"—Maury faltered— "if all the things that scared you and walked in the . . ."

Chip stared. The lights had come on in more ways than one. He realized, suddenly, why Maury had been so interested in the Spook House. He had wanted to be convinced that scary things were just phony setups. He had hoped it would chase away his fear.

But it hadn't worked. A Spook House was one thing. A sure enough Haunted House was another. Chip wanted to ask, "What is it? What is really going on in that place where you live?" But instead, he blurted out foolishly, "Could I come over Saturday? To see the cat?"

Maury gave him a swift, appraising look. "I hoped you would," he said. "Can I . . . count on you?"

Chip nodded. And they reached out solemnly to shake hands.

5

Deep in the Drink

CHIP HAD often noticed that the thing about future events was that sooner or later they became present events.

Still, he had pretended these last couple of weeks that the first day of swim class was so far away it would never really happen. He had let his mind linger only on pleasant things, like spooks. It hadn't worked. The dreaded day had arrived. This was it.

As he stood waiting just inside the Park District doors for Arnold, he tried to analyze just what there was about swimming he dreaded so much. He didn't like the screeching echoes in the locker rooms that nearly busted your eardrums. He didn't like wet concrete. He didn't like the smell of chlorine. He didn't like fumbling around without his glasses. Chip drew a deep breath. These were *minor* things. What bothered him, what really got to him, was the water itself. *He was afraid of water.*

43

He looked around, as though he had said the words aloud and been overheard.

It was a baby thing and he was ashamed to admit it even to himself. No one he knew . . . his parents, Fran, Aunt Margaret, Arnold, and other guys . . . no one else was afraid. So why was he? There must be something wrong with him. And he couldn't tell anyone. They wouldn't understand, or probably wouldn't even believe him. Who had ever heard of anyone who could swim even a little bit being afraid of water?

He was so full of dread he hardly heard Arnold's excuses for getting there at the last minute. They hurried to the locker room and out to the pool edge just as the instructor was checking off names.

"You're . . .?" The man was tall and broad shouldered.

"Sanders and Englehardt," Arnold said.

The instructor finished checking and put the notebook on a tiled ledge. Chip thought maybe he'd take off his gray sweatshirt and pants and jump into the water, but he wasn't that dumb. He was going to make the kids do it.

"My name's Alfred Wolf," he said. "Big Al, they call me, and my bite is worse than my bark. Now I gather that all you guys have had some instruction but no one's passed Beginner's. Is that right?" The boys grunted.

Big Al rubbed the back of his hand across his nose. "Then what we're going to do is spotlight your faults, correct them, and perfect your technique. By the time I'm through with you, you'll do the length of the pool and a lot more besides." He walked to the deep end, indicating with a nod of his head that they should follow. They did, none with any great enthusiasm.

"For starters," Big Al announced, "I want you to jump, here from the edge, swim out until I blow the whistle, and return. I'll be sizing you up. Lucky for you this is such a small class."

Chip muttered to Arnold, "Why is it lucky?"

"So he can zero in on every one of us."

The first boy belly-flopped and some of the kids laughed. The coach let him get out pretty far before he blew his whistle. The kid was winded by the time he dripped out of the pool, but he managed a grin.

"Next!" The second boy made a clean plunge and swam out and back. He was blond and lean and very tall. "He must be twelve, at least," Chip said.

"Yeah," Arnold agreed. "No wonder he's so good."

Chip didn't want to be last. Neither was he eager to get up there and make a spectacle of himself. He lagged along.

"Next!" Now it was his turn.

Chip curled his toes over the edge of the pool. His feet felt cold. The chill spread upward and his whole middle felt like a big block of ice, squeezed with ice tongs. The water lay spread before him, waiting. He hated it . . . he hated it! I can't do it, he thought.

"Jump!" someone called.

He couldn't turn back and face the jeers of the boys or the look on the face of the coach. He had to do it.

He clasped his fingers into fins, bent his head, and fell forward into the enemy water. Down, down, he went. There was no bottom. Gurgle, gurgle. Nothing but green, gurgly water. He kicked frantically and felt himself moving upward. It took so long! His breath was giving out. Don't breathe! He broke to the surface and gasped. Before he sank, he lashed out, but he hardly moved. His feet . . . he had to kick. He was moving now, but he couldn't remember the breathing rhythm. It was quite a while since he had swum. And he still needed air. Crack! His arm struck the water. Lift, lift, cup your hand—what else had they told him summer before last? It was hard to remember when you were on the verge of drowning. He was so tired . . . and he still had to go all the way back. Why didn't that guy blow the whistle? Maybe he had. I know, Chip thought, I'll pretend I thought I heard the whistle and turn back now. Otherwise I'll just never make it. To be rescued by Big Al was unthinkable.

Chip turned and fought his way back. Why did it take him so long to move? He was kicking and stroking all right, but the water churned. It didn't push him forward. It seemed

like twenty minutes before he neared the side
of the pool. Chip gave a lunge and grasped it as
the water lapped at his face. He edged along
the rim to the ladder with no energy at all and
got out of the pool. He could hardly stand, his
legs were so limp.

He half expected the coach to chew him out
for a lousy performance, but Big Al was already motioning to Arnold. Arnold just sort of
fell into the pool and swam as though he
couldn't care less.

"Hey, kid," one of the boys said as Chip
rejoined the group, "you came back before he
even had a chance to blow the whistle."

Chip grinned weakly. "So what? I'm not a
dog."

"Funny."

When Arnold finally pulled himself out of the
pool, the coach looked at each boy, as though
memorizing his faults.

"You," he said to the blond boy. "Peterson?
You sure you belong in this group? Repeat-
ers?" The boy nodded, eyes downcast. "Okay.
I see we have a grind ahead of us. Almost all of
you need work on your arm action. Also, I
didn't notice any great kicking. And to cap it,
your rotary breathing is for the birds. I want
you to spread out in the water now, hold onto
the edge, kick, and practice breathing. Get in
there and show me some action. Breathe as
though your life depended on it."

I really need words like that, Chip thought.
Still, he didn't mind doing it. Not as long as he

had something to hang onto. After a while the coach told them to tread water. Chip was all right for a few seconds, but as the water suddenly bobbed up to his eyes, he panicked. He struck out for the ladder just as the coach blew the whistle.

"Everybody out! See you Thursday."

In the locker room, Chip dressed quickly. "I'll wait in the hall," he told Arnold. Outside, he leaned against the wall, feeling really depressed.

"I wouldn't worry."

Chip whirled around. It was the Peterson boy.

"I'm not worried," Chip said.

"About anything. You'll make it."

Chip looked sharply at the boy. How much did he guess?

The boy gave a brief smile and left.

Chip felt a moment of calm. The Peterson boy had such a quiet air of assurance. But as Chip walked with Arnold down the corridor, heavy with the dreaded smell of chlorine, he knew it was no use. He'd never make it in swimming.

6

The First Mystery of
Maury's House

THURSDAY'S SWIM class was pretty much the same as Tuesday's . . . terrible. But at least Chip was that much closer to Saturday, and to Maury's house.

Pedaling over to Great-Aunt Clara's, Chip realized he'd have to proceed with the greatest secrecy. Agents didn't tip off anyone in advance . . . even their families. It was partly for their own protection.

Maury hadn't said much over the phone last night. Or at any other time, for that matter. He'd just hinted. That was the way it should be, at first.

If Great-Aunt Clara wondered why her nephew suddenly decided to visit, she didn't show it. "Help yourself to cookies, you know where they are," she said. "And later, when I finish up some little work around the house, we can have a nice talk."

So he could escape! "I may walk over to see

49

a boy I met around here," he said, taking several sugar cookies. "He has a new cat."

Chip had never been beyond the bushes that ringed the Gaynor yard. He glanced upward at the second story. Gray houses always had a haunty look, and this one was no exception. The weak mid-November sun glinted off the windows, so that even if spook faces watched behind them, you couldn't tell.

The small slab front porch had a weather-beaten trellis with withered vines, slightly swaying. They seemed almost to be whispering a warning.

When Chip rang the doorbell, Maury opened the door and ushered Chip directly into the living room. "It's okay, Mom," he called out. And from upstairs a voice answered, "All right, dear."

Chip looked around cautiously. The room, with its TV, sofa, and so on, was ordinary. But a dark, curving stairway toward the back gave him the creeps. It was gloomy looking now. What would it be at night?

"I'll see if I can find Rosebush," Maury said.

"Huh?"

Maury grinned. "The kitten. Oh, there he is." He scooped up the black, fluffy creature which had been dozing on a chair.

"That's really his name?" Chip asked, reaching out to pet the kitten. He would have called it Spooky, or Midnight.

"He's round and in full bloom, but just

50

watch out for the thorns," Maury said, pressing the cat's paw between his thumb and index finger to expose tiny, treacherous claws. "Here, want to hold him?"

Chip took the small animal. It immediately hooked its claws to his sweater. "They're like thorns all right." Chip rubbed his hands along the kitten's fur. It reached up and licked his chin. Its tongue was like a scrap of pink sandpaper. "I've never had a cat," he said.

"If you decide to get one, I know a girl who has plenty. Want to go up and see my room?" Maury turned toward the stairs.

Boy, did he! Chip put down the kitten and followed. The stairs were creaky *and* creepy. He practically held his breath until they entered Maury's room.

"Nice layout," Chip said politely, looking around. The walls were blue, with pennants and photographs hanging here and there. There was a desk and chair against one wall, and a window and rush-bottomed chair across the room. The wall facing the twin beds was almost entirely closet. Chip hated antiques. "You sleep in here alone?"

"Yeah," Maury said, "I used to sleep down the hall, but it was so off by itself . . . and so Alberta traded, because she isn't home much. I don't feel so . . . alone . . . now, at night. Want to see my stuff?"

"Okay," Chip said, getting up. The chair seemed to sigh.

Maury opened his closet. It lit automatically.

"There sure are a lot of lights in this room," Chip observed, looking around.

Maury seemed not to hear. "My sister's closet faces this one . . . in the next room . . ."

"How old is she?"

"Old enough for college. She goes near here. She'll be home late tonight, after some football game and dance. She doesn't come home every weekend, not because it bothers her, I mean . . ." He twitched, and looked around uneasily.

"What doesn't bother her?" Chip asked, trying to sound nonchalant.

Maury got a closed look. "Nothing. Nothing bothers Alberta. She has a very healthy outlook on life. That's what Dad says. She keeps busy at school and is in a lot of activities. She enjoys being around people, and when she's in her room, she just turns on her radio full blast and doesn't pay attention to the things . . ." Maury blinked his eyes. "Want to see the hall lights?"

"Sure. But why?"

"I'll show you."

Chip followed Maury.

"An electrician built this house. And it has a few gimmicks. See this master switch?"

Chip stared at a panel about six inches square, filled with buttons.

"These are touch-control switches for all over the house. If you are up here and want to turn on the porch light, you can do it from this panel. It controls every light, including the garage. And the button rim lights up, so you can see which lights are on. Want to try it?"

"Neat-o!" Chip pressed switches at random. Red rims went on and off.

"Maury! Is that you, playing with the lights?" A woman appeared. Her worried look was like Maury's, and so was her smile, when she saw Chip. "Oh? A friend?"

"Mom, this is Chip. He's the one . . ."

"Of course." The smile deepened. "Glad to have you here, Chip." Her glance darted to the light switch and a tiny V frown appeared between her eyes. "Those lights," she murmured. "Someday . . ."

They're a little strange at times," Maury explained. "Sometimes without anyone touching them, anyone we can see"—he glanced at his mother and a look passed between them. "They need to be adjusted," Maury amended. He pressed the last button with a rim of glowing red.

Mrs. Kinkade said, "Maury, I can't seem to locate your father's gray suit. I wonder if it could be in Berta's closet?" She smiled apologetically at Chip. "We're not quite settled yet from the move," she said. "Things are a little jumbled."

"I'll look," Maury offered. "Chip?"

They went into the room next to Maury's. Fran's room at home was fussy and ruffly, with girl junk propped every place. This room was almost bare, except for the furniture.

"Alberta took most of her stuff to school,"

Maury said. "She had some neat psychedelic posters and reams of records. This is her closet." He paused before it, and sort of stiffened. The closet, like Maury's, took up the whole length of the inner wall. Carefully, Maury reached forward and stepped back quickly as he slid the doors apart.

A couple of summery-looking dresses fluttered slightly. Maury unzipped a garment bag. Nothing inside but a girl's winter coat. The shelves had a litter of boxes and a few pairs of shoes. That was all, except for a small ladder, leaning against the wall. That must be, Chip thought, for going up through that little door in the ceiling. Maury closed the closet. "Let's go, Chip."

"It's not there, Mother," he called into her room. "C'mon, Chip, let's go downstairs."

"I'll be down in a little while and see if I can find a snack for you," Mrs. Kinkade replied. "I'd like to find that suit first. It must be here someplace."

"My Dad goes out of town a lot," Maury explained, as they went into the living room. "He's in farm machinery. We used to live in Rochester, and then, boom! Transfer. I've lived in seven states already."

"No kidding! Which states?"

Maury got a map from a bookshelf. "I'll show you." They spread it on the living room floor. Maury pointed out the city where he'd been born, and all the places he'd lived. Rosebush squirmed between them and settled himself right in the middle of the map.

Maury laughed. "I guess he wants to cover the country. Would you like to read awhile?"

"Sure." Chip felt disappointed and puzzled. Had Maury decided not to count on him? A couple of times upstairs he had seemed on the verge of saying something, but stopped. Was he afraid of talking in this house . . . or? Chip hated to think this, but could it be there really was no mystery at all? Had Maury lured him here just because he was lonesome? Chip hoped not. He'd just have to wait and see.

They lay sprawled on their stomachs, with some natural science books. Chip read one chapter about volcanoes and began the next. Maury was studying the universe. Rosebush was dozing.

Chip couldn't keep his mind on what he was reading. His eyes went over a sentence, and then back over the same sentence. Then he realized why. He was listening . . . listening to noises. Coming from the kitchen, he supposed, around the dining room. But they weren't the usual kind of continuous kitchen sounds. There was a rattling of pans, then a sort of thud. Then silence. Dead silence. No water running, no dishes rattling. In a few minutes, the same strange sounds. Just that. Then a breathless silence, as though someone hovered, listening.

Gradually, he let his eyes move to the top of

the page, and then toward Maury's shoulder, and then to his face. Maury's lips were compressed. His eyes were staring at the page in front of him. But his eyes weren't moving. His face glistened slightly with perspiration.

Chip lowered his eyes to the page. He felt prickles on his spine. Somehow, he didn't have the courage to turn around. What was going on in this house?

Then he relaxed. Of course. Mrs. Kinkade had said she was going to find a snack for them. *Find,* she had said. She was an absentminded type of mother who probably couldn't remember where she put anything. She couldn't find a suit, for Pete's sake. She probably couldn't find the cookies or pretzels or whatever she had stuck away in the cupboard, either.

Chip rotated his shoulders a little.

Maury quickly got to his knees. "Tired of reading?" he asked. "Want to go outside and ride bikes for a while?"

"Sure," Chip said.

Carefully stepping over the sleeping cat, they put the books back onto the shelves.

Chip picked up his jacket and started for the door.

"Oh, are you leaving?" a voice behind him asked.

He wheeled around.

Mrs. Kinkade smiled. "I was just going to get you something to eat."

She was coming down the stairs.

7

Something Walks
at Night

THE BOYS pedaled down the street. Chip could feel his heart pounding, and it wasn't from pumping on the bike. Finally, he could stand it no longer. He braked to a stop and balanced the bike between his legs. Maury stopped, too. His eyes, beneath the thick black hair, looked apprehensive.

Chip thought he might as well be blunt. "Who was making that noise in the kitchen?" he asked.

Maury blinked. "Oh, you heard her. I thought you did."

"It wasn't your mother."

Maury shook his head.

"And your sister and father were gone. Who was it?"

Maury bit on his lips and looked over his shoulder. Gosh, they were right on the edge of the street, away from everyone. He gave an embarrassed little laugh. "We think it's Mrs. Gaynor."

"Mrs. Gaynor? Isn't she dead?"

"Of course. She died right after they moved into that house. We think her spirit is uneasy because she never did get the place in order."

"Gosh!" Chip's body gave a sudden shiver. "A restless ghost!"

"Aw"—Maury dragged his toe back and forth on the road—"it's a kind of a family joke. Whenever something weird happens in that house, we say it's the old lady acting up again."

"What other weird things? What happens?"

"Look, Chip, if we talked about it, people would think we're crazy."

"I wouldn't."

"No, you're okay, Chip. But your folks . . . they might not let you come over if they heard some of the stories."

"They've heard rumors."

"And they let you come over anyway?"

"I didn't tell them," Chip admitted. "But listen"—he stepped to the side of the bike and began wheeling it toward his aunt's house— "grown-ups have nothing to do with kids' friendships. Right? And if you want me to be your friend, no holds barred, then you ought to spill the whole story. I've read a lot about ESP and the occult and psychic phenomena. You need support, kid. And I happen to be the one who can give it."

"I really appreciate that," Maury said warmly. "What kind of support?"

"First I'll have to find out what we're dealing with. You'd better start from the beginning. And don't spare the details." He dropped his bike on the lawn and whipped out a blue notebook and ball-point pen. The pen left a little spot of ink on his hip pocket. "Name?"

Maury's eyes crinkled. "Maurice Kinkade."

"Address?"

"Thirteen seventeen Wisteria."

"When did you move here, Mr. Kinkade?"

"About two months ago."

Now he was coming to the good questions.

"How often do you hear the sounds?"

"Which ones?"

Again, Chip felt that shiver. *Different sounds!* "Like the ones today, in the kitchen."

Maury shrugged. "A couple of times, I guess. Once when I was home alone, up in my room. I thought my mother had come back from shopping. But when I called downstairs, the sounds stopped and a little later Mom drove up. She's heard them herself. When the house is very quiet. Like today."

"Could it be"—Chip hated to risk spoiling things, but he had to be scientific—"could it be loose cupboard doors?"

"That's what my dad thought." Maury leaned against a tree. "But he tried every one of them. They have those little magnet things that keep them closed. Dad says there's some explanation. Still . . ." Maury rubbed his heel against the bark of the tree.

"Anything else?" Chip prodded. "You'd better bring me up to date."

Maury shifted. "I wonder, Chip. I appreciate your interest, but maybe we ought to leave well enough alone. I mean, there hasn't been any harm . . ."

Chip started to protest, but a guarded look in Maury's eyes stopped him. He flipped the notebook shut. "It's up to you, Maury," he said. "What I'd like to do is stake out the troubled areas."

"It's getting late and—you going to be around tomorrow?"

"No, we're having company."

Great-Aunt Clara appeared at the front door. "Your mother called, sweetheart. She wants you home before dark."

Cringing at the *sweetheart*, Chip called, "Okay."

"Thank you!" Maury called, and to Chip, "I'll phone you." He whirled away on his bike.

After apologizing to Great-Aunt Clara for staying away so long—that cat was so cute— Chip started back home.

He could hardly keep his mind on where he was going. So the rumors about the Gaynor house were true! There were things going on! Although Maury had said little, it was easy to see he was scared.

Chip knew he'd have to take it easy in several ways. His family mustn't know or they'd put a stop to his prowling about that place. He'd have to get the story out of Maury gradually because he was running scared. And instead of plunging in alone, he'd better pull Arnold into the case as a consultant. Even with his allergies and goof-off ways, Arnold had a mind that couldn't be matched for clear, scientific objectivity. Proceed with caution. That was the name of the game.

The first thing Fran asked, right in front of the family was, "How did you like the cat?"

Chip was flabbergasted. How much did they know? "What cat?" he asked warily.

"When I called, Aunt Clara said you went off with some boy who had a new kitten." Fran turned to her mother. "Couldn't we get one? You said when we got rid of the rabbits and then the gerbils . . ."

"Did I really say that? Anyway, you still have a pair of gerbils," Mrs. Sanders said. "At least it was a pair the last time I looked."

"I could sell them," Chip said, backing up his sister. "Cats are more fun. Maury's is a regular little—"

"Maury?"

"The kid down the street," he fumbled. "You know—"

Again, Fran saved him. "And cats are very clean, Mother. No cages for you . . . I mean us . . . to clean out. And they wash themselves.

And it isn't true they're aloof. If you love them, they love and respect you. Oh, I can hardly wait!"

Seeing Fran's happy face, Chip realized how much she must have wanted a cat, and how he had kept her from it by making pets of all those rodents. "You should have said something before," he mumbled.

She probably had, and he hadn't noticed. Fran wasn't so bad, even though she was a Troubled Teen-Ager. Chip considered telling her about Maury's house. It was best, though, not to spread the story around. He could hardly wait until tomorrow when he'd spring it on Arnold. It would be a real pleasure to see him good and shook up, for once!

The next day was dreary. November's first snowflakes melted against Chip's face as he went down the street.

Arnold knew a boy who would take the gerbils. "I'd keep them, myself, but I'm allergic, you know." He managed a weak sneeze.

"Are you allergic to ghosts?" Chip asked. He watched Arnold's reaction. It wasn't much.

"Not so far," Arnold commented. "But my experience has been limited."

Looking around, Chip could see why. Maury's room was a perfect setup for ghosts, with its shadowy, creaky atmosphere. Chip's room was pretty ordinary, with his projects all around and hockey and baseball clippings plastered on the walls. Arnold's room was something else. It looked like a laboratory, with its air filters, rugless floor, almost sterile desk and neatly stacked books. No self-respecting ghost would want to hang around, even if it got past the window machinery. "How about turning that thing down to low?" Chip asked.

"Okay." Arnold turned a knob on the filter and stretched out on the bed. "Now, what's this static about ghosts?"

Chip, straddling the desk chair, told Arnold how he came to meet Maury, the rumors about the house, what it looked like, and the things that had happened the day before. As he talked, Arnold's eyes got wider and wider. He sat up cross-legged on the bed.

"It looks like you're onto something," he said. He brushed at his wispy hair. "But we've got to be scientific about it."

"I thought that's what you'd say," Chip observed. "I mean, it's a good thing."

"Researchers check out everything," Arnold said. "To begin, what breed is the cat?"

"Rosebush? For Pete's sake. What's the difference?"

"Some cats are nervous by nature. Jumping in and out of places. How old is he?"

"I didn't interview the beast," Chip said, letting his annoyance show.

Arnold was unperturbed. "Maybe he was out in the kitchen, rattling things."

"Oh, no!" Chip crowed. "Rosebush was asleep, near us."

"Maybe it was the mother. She could have gone down a back stairs into the kitchen, then gone up again . . ."

"Why would she do that?"

"How should I know? I've never met the lady."

"Arnold, listen. Whether there's a back stairs or not doesn't matter. Maury was darn good and scared, the same as I was. Those sounds were spooky. And he's heard them when no one else was home."

"Don't get excited. I want to believe it. Boy, do I want to believe it. I'm just ruling out possibilities the way any expert would. Any more manifestations?"

Chip decided not to mention the footsteps on the stairs, since it might just be rumor. "Lights," he said instead. "They flick on and off."

"A short somewhere," Arnold said wisely.

"They say an electrician built the house."

Arnold swung his feet to the floor. "Why don't you give Maury a call?" he suggested. "You could ask where he got his kitten for openers. Tell him your sister wants one. Then you could work in a few other questions."

The woman who answered their call didn't sound like the mother. "Is this Maury Kinkade's house?" Chip asked.

"Right. I'm his sister."

"Oh. Could I please speak to Maury?"

She hesitated. "He's resting."

"Resting? Is he sick?"

"No. He . . . he didn't sleep much last night." She cleared her throat. "None of us did. Shall I tell him who's—oh, here he is." Chip heard her murmur and then Maury answered.

"I'm sorry, I was asleep," he said. "You see"—Chip could almost hear him breathing—"I had a little nightmare last night."

"You did?" It sounded phony.

"I guess all that talk yesterday . . ." He paused. "She's gone now. Listen, Chip"—his voice was low, but urgent—"I'm glad you're working on it, because something has to be done. It's getting worse."

Chip hunched over the phone, knuckles tightened. "Worse? How? What really happened last night?"

"They say I was dreaming. But my Mom's upset, too."

"What happened?"

"I woke up . . . and I heard it. And I was scared stiff. It wasn't the first time, you know. But this time the room was pitch-black. I know the lights were on when I went to sleep. I always leave some on. But when I heard it and woke up, every light had gone out. Or been put out."

"What happened?" Chip's voice squeaked a little.

"I heard it, there in the dark, and for a while I couldn't move. Then it got closer. I couldn't stand it. I panicked, I guess. I jumped out of bed and I think I was headed for the window. I

might have gone right out of it, but luckily, I fell. I let out a scream and the lights went on and my family came rushing in. Even Alberta woke up. My Dad went around the house and outside with a flashlight, but of course there was nothing he could find. So by the time everyone got settled down again the night was pretty well shot and no one got much sleep."

"Maury," Chip said softly, "you still haven't told me. When you were lying there in bed, in the dark, what was it that woke you up and scared you so much? What did you hear?"

Maury took a deep breath. "I heard footsteps . . . footsteps on the stairs. And then on the landing. *And they were headed for my room.*"

8

Just Psyching Myself

CHIP HURRIED to swim class Tuesday. It wasn't that he was anxious to get there. He had been thinking over Arnold's theory of the footsteps on the stairs and wanted to discuss it before the other kids showed up.

In a way, it was a shame Arnold had to be so ruthlessly scientific. But still, if you exhausted every rational idea and still there was no real explanation, then you really had something. And for Chip now, it had to be genuine spooks or no soap.

Chip looked in the corridor. No Arnold. Late again.

How had he put his theory? "Simple," he had said. "Maury was in a nervous state when he went to sleep, because of the kitchen noises earlier in the day. He was in shallow sleep when his sister Alberta came home late at night. He heard her footsteps. Those footsteps registered. He started dreaming. He redreamed the footsteps he had just heard. The dream was so real, he thought he was awake. He jumped up, still asleep, ran for the window, and luckily fell. That woke him up."

"How come," Chip had challenged, "the room was dark, when Maury had left on the lights?"

"Those master switches they have in the hall. His sister probably just jabbed at them as she rounded the corner and accidentally put out the lights in Maury's room."

Chip knew the theory made sense. But he didn't want to swallow that story. He wouldn't. Not until he checked it out himself. *In Maury's room. At night.* That's what he had to do. How, he didn't know just yet.

It really was early. The locker room was empty except for the tall, blond Peterson boy, sitting alone on a bench. He was in his swim trunks, and was leaning forward, head on his hands.

"You sick?" Chip asked hesitantly.

The boy dropped his hands, startled. When he saw it was only Chip, he gave an embarrassed little laugh. "I'm okay," he said. "Just psyching myself."

Chip liked the sound of that word. Like *sighking*. He straddled the end of the bench. "What's psyching?"

The boy looked earnestly at Chip as though to see if he could trust him not to laugh. "It means talking yourself into something. Telling yourself you can do it."

"Oh." Nothing at all. "My folks say that all the time. 'Just tell yourself you can do it.' It doesn't work."

"Yes it does!" The boy's blue eyes looked intense. "It's a state of mind, you see. I've just learned about it and I'm trying to master it. You picture yourself going down the swim lanes. In your mind, you do the strokes. You breathe in rhythm. You touch the wall and turn. You go over it in your mind . . . every action . . . perfect. And your muscles and mind are set for success."

"What if you picture yourself sinking like a stone?"

The boy's expression turned distant. "You don't picture anything like that." He turned away.

Chip felt repentant. "I'm sorry, I didn't mean . . ." He wanted to hear more.

The boy got up and left the locker room. He didn't swim nearly so well that day.

"What's the matter, Derek?" the instructor said. "You're off stride."

"I know." The boy wiped water from his face. "It happens." He didn't so much as glance at Chip. Chip felt a little guilty, but gee . . .

He didn't do well in the water, himself. In fact, he was lousy.

"I'll tell you again, Sanders," the coach said. "You'll never get anywhere until you stop regarding water as your mortal enemy."

I could feel friendly toward it if I just looked

at it the way you do, Chip thought, and never got wet.

It was like ESP in action. As though reading his mind, Big Al grabbed the back of his sweatshirt, skimmed it over his head, and poised at the edge of the pool. "Watch my technique." He arched into the pool and cut cleanly down the water, making deep, churning sounds.

Chip watched, marveling at the power of his thoughts. He glanced at Derek Peterson. The boy was watching the coach swim. Boy, was he watching. He looked as though he was memorizing every movement going on in the water. Storing it up for future psyching?

After class, as they trooped toward the locker room, Chip touched Derek lightly on the arm. The taller boy stopped and waited.

"I'm sorry if I . . . well, threw you off," Chip said. "With that remark about sinking."

The boy gave him a brief smile. "It's not your fault. I just didn't put in enough mental practice on a success pattern."

I don't think he's playing with a full deck, Chip thought. He's some kind of nut. Success pattern! Mental practice! Why didn't he just jump in and swim? No wonder Peterson still hadn't made Beginner's. Chip paused at the door. And why hadn't *he* made any progress? He didn't want to. He couldn't. And it wasn't his mental attitude, either. Or was it? He didn't want to think about it.

Although Arnold hadn't done a single thing,

Chip was grumpy all the way home. Arnold offered the cheering thought that since Thanksgiving the following week would be on Thursday, they'd get out of one swimming day. But, Chip thought, there were still two classes to go before the holiday.

On Thursday, he made a point of getting there early, not from eagerness, but to see if Derek Peterson was psyching himself again. In spite of himself, Chip was curious to see how it worked. If it did.

He was so early the blond boy was still getting dressed.

Chip thought he might as well be candid. "I came early on purpose to talk to you," he said. To himself he added, *and to find out if you really are missing a few marbles.* "I'm wondering why you think you can imagine things and make them come true."

"It works the opposite way, doesn't it? If you think, 'I'll probably get out of breath and forget how to kick,' that's what will happen. So instead, you think positively. Like, 'I'm going to cut right through the water, and surge forward, with good, solid kicks.' Your muscles respond to your mind. I should know."

"What do you mean?"

"I used to think of all the things that could go wrong. Even though I knew how to swim, by the time I jumped in, I was so full of negative thoughts I could hardly move. Then I heard about psyching. An Olympic champ did it. He did a high jump mentally, and then his muscles were all set to follow through. Believe me, it works. But you have to concentrate."

Four boys who were always together and always noisy jostled into the locker room.

Chip lowered his voice. He might never again have the nerve to ask. "Can you even psych yourself not to be afraid of the water?"

"Sure." Derek gave him an almost big-brother smile. "It's your attitude that counts. Consider the water as your friend."

Chip nodded and walked away. Friend! A friend wasn't out to drown you!

After class, the coach said, "We'll be winding up December seventeenth, which means that after today there are only seven more classes. So if we're going to pass the test we've got lots of work to do." Chip wondered why teachers always said "we have lots of work to do," when it was pretty obvious who was going to knock himself out.

His mental attitude was pretty negative right now, with that test facing him. And in just seven sessions. He just couldn't think positively about it. He wasn't going to think about it at all. There were more interesting things to brood about this coming weekend.

9

Lying in Wait

CHIP HAD decided to spend Saturday night at
Maury's. That much was certain. How he was
to do it was another matter.

The first thing he did was unload the gerbils,
at a loss, to the kid Arnold knew. Then he
made plans with Maury Saturday morning to
go have a look at the kittens.

As he pedaled to Great-Aunt Clara's he
thought of obstacles yet to come. He had said
at home that a boy near Aunt Clara's knew a
girl who had kittens. He hadn't told them about
Maury, yet he had every intention of staying
all night with him. How could he give his
family the impression he was staying at Aunt
Clara's . . . without lying? In fact, how was he
to manage permission to stay overnight at all?
He didn't even have his pajamas.

Maury solved one problem. Chip stopped
there first.

"I just called up that girl with the kittens,"
Maury apologized, "but she's going to be gone

until tonight, so we couldn't see them until tomorrow. Gee, Chip, I'm sorry you made the trip here for nothing."

"That's all right," Chip said grandly. "I'll stay the night with you."

"You will?" Maury looked surprised, but pleased.

"I'll just buzz off," Chip said, "to say hello to my relatives." He had thought of a plan. He hoped his Aunt Margaret would be out tonight. He could fool Great-Aunt Clara, but the young aunt was something else again.

Before leaving, he checked out the section of roof outside Maury's window. Good. It was flat. Just right for his scheme. "Do you happen to have a ladder?" he asked. "One that reaches up to that roof?"

"Sure. In the garage."

"Maybe we could haul it out."

Maury smiled pleasantly. "But what for?"

"We may need it," Chip said mysteriously. "I'll be right back."

"Good. I have some new things to tell you."

Aunt Clara was less delighted than Maury had been when Chip announced once more he was spending the night. He explained the kitten situation.

"Sweetheart, I love your company, but tonight I'll be busy. It's my turn to have some club ladies over."

"Aunt Clara, I'd stay in the room." Chip

was careful not to state exactly which room. "I wouldn't be lonesome. In fact, I'd be glad. Please?"

"All right, sugar. I know how children like to visit overnight. And how you like to read until all hours," she added with a teasing smile.

When she offered to call his parents to tell them she'd invited him to stay overnight, Chip didn't remind her that he had invited himself.

Chip went back to Maury's and explained why he wanted the ladder. "It will be my secret entrance and exit to your room," he said. Maury nodded. "It's always best in these situations to let as few people in on it as possible. Not only on account of the spook angle, but because your parents might sometime accidentally mention I've been here." Maury nodded once more.

"What we have to do this afternoon is set up signals. So when I slip up the ladder tonight and tap at your window, you'll know who it is."

Maury nodded. "Let's be sure to get the signals straight. What's the code?"

"I'll rap once. Then pause. Three quick raps. Pause. Then two. Got it?"

"Let's go through all the motions. I'll go up and climb through the window into my room and wait for your signal."

They practiced several times.

"Did you bring your notebook, Chip?" Maury asked, when they were out in the yard again. "I have more things to tell you."

It took a lot of willpower to answer, "Let's wait until tonight."

Aunt Margaret excused herself right after dinner. "I'll be home late," she said. "After the ladies have gone. Leave the dishes, Mother. I mean it."

When he was sure she had driven away, Chip said, "I guess I'll go upstairs now."

"So early?" Aunt Clara peered into the refrigerator. "Now, where did I put those olives?"

"Aunt Clara . . . if my door is closed and the light is out, you won't check on me, will you?"

"Of course not. You're not a baby. Take some of those little sandwiches and cookies along so you don't starve before morning."

Chip carried them upstairs on a plate and then crammed as many as he could into his pockets. Then he tiptoed back down the stairs and listened until he heard his aunt busy in the kitchen. He glided into the living room and quietly opened the front door. Then he dashed down the street to Maury's.

In the backyard, Chip looked carefully around, to see if he had been tailed. Then he crept cautiously up the ladder and slid on his stomach across the roof and to the window. He rapped once. Pause. Three raps. Pause. Two.

Maury's smiling face appeared at the window. He raised it for Chip to climb through.

"Any trouble?"

"Naw. I told you there wouldn't be."

"Won't they miss you?"

"I doubt it." Chip explained the situation. "I even brought us some chow." He pulled the food, not mashed much, out of his pockets and shared it with Maury.

"Now the time is right," Chip said, sitting cross-legged on one of the beds, "to bring me up to date. What new things did you have to tell me?"

Maury gave an apprehensive glance at the shadowy corners of the room and hunched a little forward on the bed opposite Chip. "My mother met a Mrs. Valkyrie."

"So?" Chip twisted his hand to lick off a glob of sandwich filling.

"She lived in this house for a while."

"No kidding! And what did she have to say?"

"At first—I was with Mom—this woman just hinted around, asked how we like the house and all. Then finally she gave a kind of forced laugh and asked if we'd got used to the noises."

"Did she say what kind of noises?"

"Yes, because my Mom played dumb. So Mrs. Valkyrie came right out and said, '*Cupboard doors, footsteps on the stairs.*' "

Chip straightened. "That woman heard them too?"

"Not only that. She made special mention of the closet in Berta's room. Footsteps going back and forth in there. And she said something else . . .''

Chip leaned forward. "What?"

"She said it's worse in the fall. Late fall." Maury's eyes were dark and enormous. "Like this time of year."

"My gosh!" Chip almost tumbled forward. "So I guess you weren't dreaming."

"Of course I wasn't dreaming! Not last Saturday night nor Tuesday night."

"Tuesday? You didn't tell me about that."

"I tried to, this afternoon, remember? But you said to wait until tonight."

"I know. I like to set the mood. But Maury, tell me. What happened? Tell everything!"

"I was in bed . . ."

"And the lights went out?"

"Not this time. But they came anyway, the footsteps. Into this room!"

Chip took a deep breath. "Right here?"

Maury nodded. "Across the room, to that chair over there. Boy, I was scared stiff. And, Chip, it wasn't just the footsteps that were so terrible. There was a sudden blast of cold, like when you open the refrigerator. No, worse. It just seemed to go right through me."

"And what happened next?" Chip was shivering right now.

"I don't know how long it took, maybe it was a few minutes, but it could have been longer, I was frozen stiff. The footsteps passed by the beds again and out the door. Next, I heard them go down the hall—the boards creak a little, you know—and then into Alberta's room. And the closet doors opened and there were sounds in her closet."

"What kind of sounds?"

"Bangings on the wall and a kind of scraping on the floor. And then it was quiet."

"What did you do?"

"Do? Nothing. I was petrified." Maury's eyes were round and staring. "Wouldn't you be?"

Chip considered. He wanted to be honest. "I'd be shook up, some," he confessed. "But most of all, boy, I'd want to find out what was going on. I'd sure like to hear those footsteps!"

"You may get a chance," Maury said. "Tonight."

"Then let's not waste any more time talking," Chip decided. "Let's turn out the lights and lie in wait."

"Couldn't we leave the lights on?" Maury asked.

"It might hurry things up if it was dark," Chip said. "I can't stick around too long tonight." He was sorry now he hadn't come right out and asked to stay at Maury's. Instead of being able to give all his attention to the ghost, he was worried about being found out.

Maury changed into his pajamas and Chip stretched out on the bed, fully dressed, with a magazine under his shoes to protect the bedspread.

The room was a black tunnel at first. Gradually, as Chip's eyes got used to the dark, he could make out shapes of objects. A thin light sifted from outside. "Shouldn't we open the window a little?" Chip asked.

"We could, but . . ." Maury paused. "The roof's flat, remember, and we left the ladder leaning against it . . . so . . ."

"Oh." Lying there, Chip felt very sorry for Maury. Such a nice kid, but so *afraid*. Ghosts, prowlers . . . what else? It must be terrible to have fear. The idea of burglars didn't bother *him*. They only went to rich houses anyway. And as for spooks . . . he'd give his eyeteeth just to see how they operated. He felt only curiosity, not fear. He was afraid of nothing.

A sudden thought made him shift. Water. He was afraid of water. But that was something else. Water was deep, and menacing. It lay there in wait like—*what was that sound?*

He raised his head slightly and listened. Nothing. Although he couldn't see Maury, he could almost feel the tenseness of him, lying there in the other bed. Chip gave a fake yawn and began breathing deeply, to sort of soothe his poor, worried friend. He decided to think of something restful. A vacation his family took one year. Yes. A summer cottage near a shallow, sandy beach. Night breezes and the soft swish of leaves outside the screened porch where he was lying. Low, soothing night sounds . . . away . . . away.

Suddenly he jerked as Maury whispered, "Chip!" Had he been sleeping?

83

"What is it?" The drowsiness dissolved. "What, Maury?"

"Noises." Maury's voice was barely audible. "Outside."

Chip raised his head, alert. "In the hall?"

"On the roof. Sssssss.

Chip listened. Something against the side of the house . . . and then a soft sound, almost a whimper. He quietly put his feet on the floor.

"Where are you going?" Maury's voice was breathy, frightened.

"To investigate." Chip dropped on all fours and crawled through the darkness toward the dim light of the window.

"Be careful!" Although breathing heavily, Maury dropped to the floor behind him.

Cautiously, Chip made his way to the window. He flattened himself against the wall beside it, and then slowly moved his head so that one eye could peer outside. Blackness. He squinted. Gradually, he could make out a small, dark shape. It moved. It came closer. He pulled back slightly.

"Meow." It was a pitiful, weak sound.

Together, the boys gasped, "Rosebush!"

"Meow!"

"Oh, the poor kitten!" Maury raised the window and scooped up his pet. "He's been out there on the roof ever since we closed the window. Rosebush!" He buried his face in the cat's fur.

Chip reached up and flicked on the desk

lamp. He was glad the cat was okay, but boy, what a letdown! His eyes swept across the clock and returned with a jolt. "Maury! Look at the time! Two A.M.! I've got to blast out of here."

"Okay," Maury said agreeably, scratching Rosebush under the chin. "Think you'll get into trouble?" he asked sympathetically. "I could go along with you and help explain."

"Naw," Chip said, trying to act nonchalant. "I'll manage."

"Come back over Thanksgiving, if you can," Maury said, seeing him out the window. "There's sure to be some action then."

There'll be some action tonight, Chip thought, if I'm caught. He gave a wave and felt his way down the ladder.

He wasted no time jogging down the dark street. What if they had discovered him missing and had called the police—or called his folks!

He came within sight of Aunt Clara's. What a relief. Everything was dark and silent. The cars were gone. The garage door was closed. Aunt Margaret must be home.

He tiptoed up the front steps. He carefully turned the knob. The door was locked.

Now his heart started triple beating. He crept around to the back door. Locked. What could he do? He was shivering, but not from the November cold. He looked up to the second-floor windows. High. It was too dark and difficult to go drag Maury's ladder here. And if he opened the garage doors here, they'd be alerted.

He couldn't just stand there. He had to get in. If he only had a key!

Then he remembered. There was one. Left outside purposely in case Chip's family happened by while no one was home. In the flowerpot under the back step.

Be there! Chip grabbed so fast the flowerpot fell over. There was a *cling* on the cement. Chip felt around until his fingers closed onto the key.

Shaking, he fitted it into the lock and . . . whew! The door eased open. Warmth . . . safety! He closed the door slowly behind him and tiptoed through the kitchen with its small light over the sink, and slowly, slowly up the stairs.

Huddled in bed in his underwear a few minutes later, he made a decision. He just couldn't take a chance like this again. He'd never hear the end of it if he turned up missing. And it would also mean curtains to the great ghost hunt. He'd simply have to tell his family about Maury.

10

All in the Mind?

CHIP MANAGED to see the kittens the next day. When he got home he described them to his family.

"There's one fluffy one," he said. "White, with a black tail that looks like a plume, and black front paws. It's real loving, like Rosebush."

"Rose *who?*" Mrs. Sanders asked.

"Rosebush," Chip said with a sigh, "is the name of Maury's cat."

"And who is Maury?"

"That kid down the street from Aunt Clara's. Who knows the girl who has the kittens."

"Oh, yes," Mrs. Sanders said, absentmindedly, picking up strewn Sunday papers.

Chip thought he might as well take the plunge. "Could I stay overnight with Maury Thanksgiving? We'll be at Aunt Clara's for dinner anyway, so you wouldn't have to drive me, in case it snows . . ."

"How does it happen we've never met him?" Mr. Sanders asked.

"Maury? He just moved, not so long ago. To that gray house on the corner."

"The Gaynor house?" His father glanced quickly at Mrs. Sanders, then back at Chip. "You're a boy who believes in ghosts. Aren't you afraid of that place at night?"

"Oh, Ed, don't frighten him," Mrs. Sanders said.

Mr. Sanders grinned. "Are you frightened, Chip?"

"Naw. Can I go, Dad?"

"It's all right with me. Maybe you boys can convince the neighborhood gossips that it's just an ordinary house."

"A little child shall lead them," Fran said. Chip punched her.

Mrs. Sanders frowned. "Chip, I'm not so sure it's a good idea. After the other night . . ."

Chip's heart sank. Had he been found out? He followed his mother to the kitchen. "What is it?"

He waited apprehensively while she stepped out to the garage to dump the papers. "You screamed in your sleep." She looked him straight in the eye. "Are you reading mystery stories late at night? You seem tired out and jumpy."

He didn't feel jumpy now. He was breathing a sigh of relief. "I haven't done any such thing," he said honestly. "I've just been dreaming a lot."

She brushed his cheek. "Are you worried about something?"

Chip felt tempted to tell her he was worried about his swimming test. But that wasn't true. He didn't even think about it. "I have a lot on my mind," he said.

"School?"

"Gosh, no!" That was the last thing he'd dream about. It was enough during the day.

"Then what?"

"I know." Fran stood in the doorway, smiling wisely. "It's all those little sounds. That aren't there."

Chip stared at her. The traitor! And how had she found out? "What do you mean?" he stammered.

She laughed. "Just kidding. The patter of little feet. Mice feet. Gerbil feet. It seems so quiet around here without any little pets. Could we go see the kitten today, Mother? Right away? Please?"

Mrs. Sanders, who now had a glass of water in her hand, looked as though she might pour it over her head. "If you two don't stop nagging me," she said, *"I'll* go somewhere. Right smack out of my mind."

Chip had to get it settled. "May I go to Maury's?"

"Go," his mother said. "Stay Thanksgiving night. And Fran, you'll have to wait until then to get that kitten. Right now, you two can do me a favor by going outside."

Getting into her jacket, Fran whispered, "It

worked. I thought it would be ages before they'd break down."

If it hadn't been for Veronica, who came along to Great-Aunt Clara's for Thanksgiving, Chip could hardly have sat through the meal. Veronica always kept things lively.

Maury had promised to bring Fran's kitten over later that afternoon. Chip thought, I hope he doesn't say anything to spoil my chances of sleeping over. It didn't seem likely.

The time finally came. Everyone admired the creature.

"Chip," Mrs. Sanders said, when the girls, with Maury trailing, went to the kitchen to pour some milk, "I had no idea he was so nice. I'm so glad you found him."

"It's a girl cat," Chip corrected.

"I meant Maury."

For Pete's sake. Chip nodded and went out to join the others.

Fran was squatting on the floor beside the kitten, dipping her finger into the milk in encouragement.

"Does it catch mice?" Veronica asked, sitting on a counter, legs dangling.

"Not yet. It's too young."

"Then I'm going to round up an older cat somewhere. I heard a mouse in our cupboard the other day. Might as well give some cat a good meal."

"That's revolting," Fran said.

"How do you know it's a mouse?" Maury asked cautiously.

"What else could it be?" Veronica kicked her heels slightly against the cupboard. One side sprang open. "You know," she said, easing the door until it clicked into place, "I used to be so gullible."

"You?" Fran tilted up her head and smiled.

"No kidding. Everything scared me. Take movies. Whenever I'd see a plane shot down or a building blown up, for instance, I'd lie awake nights, thinking about those poor people. Then one day I happened to mention it to my Gramma Alice and she really laughed, and set me straight."

"How *do* they do it?" Fran asked.

"They use models of the real thing and blow them up. They wouldn't *kill* anyone just to make a movie. No one even gets hurt, unless it's by accident."

"I've seen fight scenes, though," Chip said, "where guys really got bloodied up."

"Trick photography. All done by cutting and splicing films. They show a guy swinging, and then cut to a shot of someone staggering, maybe with blood pouring out of his nose. Well, that blood is fake, and no one really hit him. You think you saw it, but it's all in the mind."

It's all in the mind. Is there really a logical explanation for everything? Chip wondered. But Veronica was talking about movies. That

91

was a business. It had nothing to do with the occult. Chip was getting a little bored with all this girl and cat chatter. He wanted to get the latest lowdown on the Gaynor house goings-on. "Let's go outside," he suggested, grabbing his jacket. Maury nodded.

When they rounded the corner of the house, Chip clutched Maury's arm. "Any more ghost noises?" he asked softly.

Maury's face suddenly lost its carefree look. "Almost every night now. It's terrible. We kind of kid about it, but I know my Mom is upset. Berta's home this week and of course she hears it too, since most of the commotion is right in her room."

"Is she real shook up?"

"Not Alberta. It just makes her mad."

"Mad?"

"Yeah. My sister likes to go her own way without interference. The ghost makes Berta mad because it sometimes walks when Berta wants to sleep."

"I see." Maury's sister sounded like a real winner. "You still scar . . . upset, Maury?"

"I sure am. Chip, you've got to crack this case soon. It's really getting to me."

"I'll have to get a fix on that spook first. I sure hope it walks tonight."

"It will." Maury shivered. "I feel it in my bones."

11

If the Spirit Grabs You!

To KILL time, and to build up their muscles, the boys kicked and passed the football in the front yard. The sun, partly obscured by mist, hung low in the sky. Finally, tired from their exercise, they slumped on the steps, breathing deeply of the chill, late autumn air. For the past hour, Chip had had his mind only on football technique. Now, as the day drew to a close, he thought of the evening and of what it might bring.

"That Val . . . woman . . . the one who used to live in your house?" he ventured.

"Valkyrie."

"Yeh. Did she ever meet Mrs. Gaynor? Before she died, I mean?"

"Oh, no. All she knew was from rumors. They said . . . other people who lived in the house . . . that the story was Mrs. Gaynor dropped dead after she lived in the house for a couple of days. Heart trouble. She wasn't supposed to exert herself. No heavy lifting or stairs or things like that."

"Then why," Chip asked, "did she have a two-story house?"

"She just wanted one. Mrs. Gaynor was a stubborn woman. And feisty. That's what they say."

Chip frowned. There was something rumbling around in his mind. Something about the house. Mrs. Gaynor had it built to order. Built . . . built. Suddenly he knew. "Maury! You told me, that first day I went to your house, an electrician built it."

"That's right. Mr. Gaynor."

"With all those remote control switches."

"Yeah. I guess it was to save his wife from going up and down those stairs so much."

Chip stared at his friend thoughtfully. There was some connection: stairs, light switches. Heart trouble. But what?

"I'm cold," Maury said. "Shouldn't we go in?"

After a while, Mr. and Mrs. Sanders and the girls left, after Chip promised to be ready to be picked up the next day at about noon, and not to bother Great-Aunt Clara, who would need her rest after the excitement of the holiday.

The boys went to Maury's and watched TV for a while. Chip wasn't hungry, but he obligingly kept Maury company with a turkey sandwich, Jello and a piece of pumpkin pie, out in the kitchen at about nine o'clock.

Chip still hadn't met Mr. Kinkade because

Maury's parents had gone to a play in the city. Alberta was home, though. She was just like Maury said. Very sure of herself, speaking in a loud, hearty voice about all the goings-on at college. She was a cheer leader. Chip could see why. Her voice sure did carry, and her actions were very direct and final, like the way she slammed the refrigerator door and turned on water full blast. The dishes rattled when she walked across the room. She must take after her father, Chip thought, because she was big and blond, while both Maury and his mother were brown eyed, dark haired, and gentle.

Still, Chip liked Alberta. She cheerfully plunked the dishes into the sink, and rinsed them through a stream of water while she described some of the more exciting games of the season.

"Okay, that ties it," she said finally, dropping the garbage into the pail with a thud. "I've got to shag upstairs and hit the books or I'll flunk math for sure. Dig you clams later." She went up the stairs whistling and soon, from her room in the far reaches of the house, sounds of a rock tune on a radio came thumping.

"We might as well lock up and go to bed," Maury said. "My folks won't be home until real late. They're going out with some people after the play."

Chip followed Maury around, relieved to see the house was securely locked. If he heard anything walking around in the night, he wanted to be sure it was a ghost.

Going up the stairs, he clapped his hands over his ears as the music boomed louder and louder. He wondered how the family could stand it. Maury seemed not to notice. "Come, Rosebush," he coaxed, scooping up the kitten. "You come with us tonight, and no tricks."

Chip felt excited, and yet geared for disappointment. Maury's folks were gone, the night was chill and dark, it was the right season of the year, and the ghost was making almost nightly visits. Yet, would any spirit venture into a house that was shaking on its foundation from rock tunes?

He got undressed while his head reeled. Those closets must be pretty thin. They carried sound like anything. "Shouldn't she turn down the volume a little while she's studying?" he finally asked Maury.

"It keeps her going. She can't concentrate when it's quiet." Maury reached for a stack of *Mad* magazines and offered Chip a few. They sat in bed, reading. Suddenly, the sound from the next room snapped off. Chip looked up, alarmed.

Maury yawned and turned a page. "She's asleep."

"Asleep?"

"She konks out"—Maury snapped his fingers—"like that."

"Is she finished with her math already?"

"She has all weekend," Maury pointed out. "Berta needs a lot of sleep. She expends a lot of energy." He yawned again. "I wish I could fall asleep like she does. I think I'm tired, but then I lie awake. It's annoying."

"You tired now?"

"Not really. Are you?"

"Not really. I guess I'm like you. I don't think I could fall asleep for quite a while tonight, for instance."

"Oh well. There's plenty to read."

Chip leafed through a couple of more magazines and then went to the bookcase and pulled out an adventure novel. Maury reached for a book at his bedside. It was eleven o'clock.

Chip's book was about a shipwreck and how a few survivors made it to an island. He read on and on. He was about a third of the way through the book when he suddenly stirred and glanced at the clock. Twelve thirty! He shifted to see if Maury was asleep in the other bed. Maury was staring at him, wide eyed. Chip gave a start.

"What's the matter?" he asked, and in that instant knew something was about to happen.

"Didn't you hear it?" Maury whispered.

"What?"

"Listen!"

Chip quickly snapped off the light, explaining, "It gives us better cover." Tense now, he strained, looking at the closed door where Maury's eyes were focused. Nothing. Then . . . from a distance, a slight shuffling sound. Maury didn't move.

Chip held his breath, straining to hear. Yes . . . there was a sound . . . a slight sound . . . on the stairway.

Your folks? Chip wanted to say, but he couldn't form the words. His eyes, now accustomed to the dark, were focused on the closed door.

The shuffling continued, step by step, louder now, and closer.

Then there was silence, more frightening than sound. It was as though the house and everyone in it was holding its breath. Chip's body felt like one big, fast heartbeat. *There was something on the landing. Waiting.*

The bedroom door sort of quivered. As Chip watched, unable to move or utter a sound, it opened. He felt a whimper deep in his throat, but it didn't come out. *What was going to happen?*

Footsteps. Into the room and along the foot of Maury's bed—and no! Coming across. Now at the foot of his bed! An icy coldness swept toward him. He shook, wide eyed and frozen. The steps continued, then paused at the rush-bottomed chair. As Chip stared, there was a rustly sound. His eyes traveled up, to where a face must be . . . gazing at him. In a moment, the chair creaked. Again, the coldness like a blast of zero weather, and footsteps along the foot of his bed, and then across. They went out into the hall through the open door. Chip took in a great gulp of air and looked at Maury. The boy was sitting, clutching handfuls of sheet.

"My gosh!" Chip breathed. "My gosh!"

"Sssssssh. Listen." Maury leaned slightly forward.

Then Chip heard it. In the next room, Alberta's room. This time there was more than footsteps. There was a sound like wood against wood.

"It's in the closet," Chip exclaimed, staring at the one in this room.

"She always heads there. I told you," Maury whispered, listening intently. "That's where she makes the most racket."

The sounds increased now, moving up and down the wall, as though they would burst right through. There was a low, whistling sound, like wind in a tunnel.

Although Chip's heart was still pounding and every instinct told him to stay right where he was, he lifted the covers from his legs and swung them to the side of the bed. He had to see how those sounds were being made. He would go into the next room and look in the closet!

His toes touched the floor. He hoisted himself up . . . and landed on the floor in a heap as a sudden sound blasted from Alberta's room. Her radio!

"You all right?" Maury switched on the light and peered at him anxiously.

"What's with your sister?" Chip exclaimed. "Why did she turn that darn radio on at a time like this?"

"She always does," Maury explained. "I

told you that ghost makes Berta mad. It interferes with her sleep. The radio drives Mrs. Gaynor away."

"I can see why," Chip said, disgusted. He eased onto the bed, listening. In a few minutes, the radio went off. But there were no more sounds from the closet. The ghost was gone.

12

More About Mrs. Gaynor

"YOU'RE PUTTING me on," Arnold said.

"No, I'm not!" Chip's heart beat rapidly, just telling about it. "I actually heard it. And so did Maury. Didn't you?"

Maury nodded solemnly.

It was Friday afternoon, the day after Thanksgiving. Maury had come home with Chip, and the boys had wasted no time getting Arnold over to the house.

"You're sure it wasn't your folks." It was a statement, not a question. Although Arnold's detached scientific mind was annoying at times, Chip had to respect the way he never let emotion get the better of him. He was a valuable part of the team for this reason, and an inspiration.

Chip flipped open his notebook. "We've checked out every theory," he stated. "Folks weren't home. We checked rooms and locks. Also, we heard them when they did get back."

"And they wouldn't play tricks just to . . ."

Arnold floundered. It wasn't the sort of trick parents would play, even on ornery kids.

"No offense," he said to Maury. "I withdraw the question."

Maury nodded agreeably.

"It wasn't Alberta," Chip continued, putting a check mark next to the sister's name.

"Proof?" Arnold prodded.

"We just know," Chip protested.

"Not good enough." Arnold fixed them with a stare.

Chip's thoughts were confused. Gosh, if he were ever on a witness stand! Ideas tumbled through his mind like clothes in a dryer. There were noises in Alberta's closet . . . but she could have tramped around herself . . . and then, boom, turned on the radio!

"The door opened," Maury said mildly. "Footsteps came into our room and something sat on the chair. It wasn't my sister. We sure could have seen her."

"I'll say!" Chip exclaimed. "Alberta is one big chunk of a girl."

"There was someone in the room, then," Arnold stated. "But not a corporeal being."

"Huh?"

"A human. A live person," Arnold explained with just a shade of superiority.

"It was spooksville," Chip said, annoyed. "A ghost for sure."

"The cat?" Arnold persisted.

"Oh come on," Chip said angrily. "Rosebush was right in the room, and besides, I could see him if he walked across the room and sat on a chair. Don't be dense, Englehardt."

"So what do we do now?" Maury asked diplomatically. "We've established the fact that it's a ghost. Right?"

"Right," Chip said.

"Perhaps," Arnold said.

Maury bit his lip. "Then I guess that's all there is to it. We can't do anything about it. Can we?"

"Maury," Chip said, "you don't mean to tell me you're throwing in the towel?"

The boy shrugged. "What can we do?"

"We can exorcise the ghost."

"Exercise?" Arnold wrinkled his brow. "You mean, like a dog?"

"Ex-*or*-cise, you dope," Chip said, pleased to be one up on Arnold. "Exorcise means to get rid of."

"But how can we?" Maury wanted to know.

"There are ways." Chip folded his arms and frowned as though deep in thought. The boys waited respectfully. "Any number of ways." Again, Chip felt as though he were on the witness stand. Fragments of things he had read drifted through his mind. *Ghosts were supposed to be afraid of lights.* Maury's ghost wasn't. *Ghosts can be seen in a mirror, over your shoulder.* The idea, though, was to get rid of it. *Call them by name and they'll disappear.* He straightened. "Did you ever call the ghost 'Mrs. Gaynor' right to her . . . uh . . .face?" he asked Maury.

"I . . . I . . ." Maury's tongue seemed paralyzed even at the thought.

"I'll make a note of it," Chip said. He had another thought. A winner this time. "You can trap ghosts by strewing ashes!" he burst out. "I read that in an anthology." Why hadn't he thought of that before? "We could strew ashes on the floor of Alberta's closet and see the footprints . . . or ridges, or whatever they make." He was really in orbit now.

Arnold sneezed.

"For Pete's sake," Chip said, drawing back. "Don't tell me you're allergic to ashes. Even the thought of them?"

"I have a cold," Arnold said mildly. "Can't you tell by my voice? I really shouldn't be out."

What a martyr. But Arnold's voice *was* deeper than usual. Chip turned to Maury. "Would you be willing to sprinkle a few ashes in Alberta's closet? As long as she doesn't use it much anyway?"

"Sure. If the ghost of Mrs. Gaynor leaves a footprint will that scare her off the premises?"

"I don't have that information," Chip faltered. "But even if it didn't wouldn't it be something to see?"

Everyone agreed a ghost's footprint would be a real thrill.

Arnold strolled to Chip's desk where he helped himself to a Kleenex. Just in time. When the echoes of the sneeze died down, he stated, "It seems to me there are other areas to work on in exorcising the ghost." He used the word as though he had known it for years. "Things we could do some more work on."

"Like what?" Chip challenged.

"Review your notes," Arnold suggested. "Something may pop up that we've overlooked before."

Chip flipped open the small notebook. "An account of Maury's dream, which we later found out was no dream . . . mmmm." He turned a few pages. "Cupboard doors . . ."

"You've checked that one out?" Arnold asked. "No one out there when they slam?"

"No one."

Chip continued. "Closet. Why *that* closet?" He felt there was something he had once noticed. But what?

"Is your sister's closet like yours?" Arnold asked Maury.

"Sure. They're back to back. But she . . . the ghost . . . never goes into mine. Just Alberta's."

"Maybe Mrs. Gaynor died in there," Arnold observed. "Maybe she hanged herself. On a hanger," he added, smiling feebly.

"She died of a heart attack," Maury said. "At least, that's what I heard."

"Maybe that's just a cover-up story. For something grisly."

"If so, no one's still telling," Maury said. "But maybe we could find out."

"How?" Chip reluctantly pulled his attention from the thought of the closet.

"Newspapers," Maury said simply. "They give the real scoop."

Arnold gave a small, patient sigh. "Mrs. Gaynor died any number of years ago. People don't keep papers that long."

"The library does," Maury said.

There was total silence. Then Chip and Arnold gave a whoop.

"Old boy," Chip said, pulling his friend by the elbow, "we've struck pay dirt!"

"There's only one thing," Maury said with a slow smile. "What year? We could spend all day . . ."

"Then we will," Arnold said briskly. "No one ever said research was easy."

No one, Chip thought, ever said you had to spend a whole vacation going through old newspapers, either. There must be an easier way. "Just a minute." He retreated deep into thought, wincing as Arnold took the opportunity to sneeze. "I've got it. Call Mr. Gaynor."

Arnold eyed him. "You mean, just like that. 'Hello, Mr. Gaynor, I'm a kid. I just thought I'd call you up to ask you when your wife croaked.' "

"I thought of the idea," Chip challenged. "You think of a way to do it."

"We could pretend to be census takers," Maury suggested. "No, that's no good."

"Carpet salesman?" Arnold suggested. "Ask to speak to the lady of the house? No, he'd just say there wasn't any."

Suddenly, in his mind's eye, Chip saw the

electrical switches in Maury's house. "I've got it!" he shouted. "Mr. Gaynor was an electrician. Maybe he still is, for all we know. We could pretend to be worried about the switches. You know you have trouble with them, Maury. We could ask Mr. Gaynor what year they were installed so we could track down parts for them from the factory."

"Yeah . . ." Arnold agreed. "Even if we sounded dumb, it wouldn't matter. Most people don't know beans about electricity."

"If we found out the year the house was built," Maury added, "we'd be right on the track, because Mrs. Gaynor died right after they moved in."

They threw their arms around each other's shoulders and gave a shout. "Where's the phone book?" Arnold asked, breaking away.

"In the kitchen."

The list of Gaynors in the book was long, and they didn't know his first name.

"Let's do it the easy way," Chip said. "Call the electric companies."

"Right! The yellow pages." Arnold flipped to the section. "Contractors, not companies," he corrected. "There are only seven of them. Who's going to call?"

"You," Chip said. "You have the lowest voice. They'll never know it's a kid if you don't giggle."

"I never giggle." Arnold dialed a number. "May I speak to Mr. Gaynor?" he asked. "Sorry." He hung up. "No one by that name working there," he reported. "I'll try the next one." He got the same response. It happened two more times. The fifth time, he gulped and murmured, "Yes, I'll hold on." He clamped his hand over the mouthpiece. "They're going to get him." His eyes blinked. "What'll I say?"

"Find out if it's the same Gaynor," Chip hissed. "Don't blow it."

Arnold removed his hand. "Uh, yes." He listened. "Yes, that's who I mean. Oh, is that so? What was that first name again? Thanks!" He hung back the phone and heaved a sigh. He looked pale, except for a strange flush on his cheeks.

"What happened?" the boys asked in unison.

"Joe Gaynor left the firm a couple of years ago. Joe." He flicked to the alphabetical listing. "Here he is . . . *Gaynor, Joseph P.*" He looked up. "Shall I?"

"Go ahead."

He dialed and waited. The phone rang several times. "I guess he's not . . . oh, hello." In his excitement, Arnold's voice raised. He swallowed. "Mr. Gaynor? Is this the electrician? I'm calling about that house you wired on . . ."

"Wisteria Street," Maury prompted.

"Wisteria Street. Having a little trouble with those switches." His voice was deep and confident now. "They go off and on. Understand you built that house. Could you tell me when you installed the switches?" He frowned.

"November of what *year*, Mr. Gaynor? You sure?" Holding his hand over the mouthpiece he hissed, "November, nineteen seventy-one. . . . Oh?" He listened intently, fluttering his lashes slightly. "I'm sorry to hear that. What did she die of? What? No difference, Mr. Gaynor, just taking a friendly interest." He rolled his eyes. "Thanks." He hung up. "Whew!"

"What happened?"

"He said it was none of my business what his wife died of."

Chip patted his back. "Anyway, you got the information. Imagine . . . she died in November. No wonder her spirit is so restless this time of year."

"I hope Mr. Gaynor wasn't upset," Maury said. "But I'm sure he didn't suspect anything. You're so cool, Arnold."

"I feel a little feverish."

"I really admire your nerves of steel. Yours too, Chip."

"I didn't talk on the phone."

"No, but I keep remembering how you reacted the other night when the ghost walked. If Alberta hadn't scared off the spook you'd have gone right in there after it. Now, if that isn't cool courage, I don't know what is."

"I just don't believe in holding back," Chip said. "If there's something you've got to do, it's better to plunge right in." A sickening thought of the pool washed over him. He glanced furtively at the boys to see if they suspected what a phony he was, but they seemed lost in thoughts of ghosts.

Since Maury didn't have his bicycle, they had to walk the several blocks to the library. It was awfully cold outside, and dreary, as though there might be snow that night. Arnold was wheezing by the time they got there. His face looked pinched and white. He stood inside the entrance, coughing and shivering.

"You'd better get out of the draft," Chip said, ushering him away from the open door. "You okay, Arnold?"

"Yeh."

He didn't look good at all. Chip was so used to his friend's sneezing and everything he hadn't paid much attention today. Now he was sorry they had come to the library. "Maybe we ought to call your mother to come get you," he suggested.

"I tell you, I'm all right." He sneezed. "Come on, let's ask the librarian about the old newspapers."

Mrs. Hoephner, a tall, salt-and-pepper-haired lady, was on duty. She seemed only mildly surprised at their request. "Just give me a few minutes to go dig in the archives," she said. "I haven't had a request like this in years." She smiled and disappeared.

The papers, when she brought them, were in a giant loose-leaf folder. "Just put it back on the counter when you're finished, please." She went back to her typing.

They went through the first two weeks of November 1971. The obituary columns, toward the back of the paper, were awfully dull. They finished the third week and started on the fourth. And then they saw it. *Loretta Gurlie Gaynor, 55, beloved wife of Joseph Gaynor, dear sister of* . . . and so forth.

"Gee," Chip said with a disappointed sigh, "that doesn't tell us much."

Arnold wiped his forehead, which was moist. "Maybe there's a news item, too," he said. "There was one for my grandfather when he died."

They searched through the paper. "Here!" Chip almost shouted, forgetting where he was. *"Loretta Gaynor Succumbs in Home.* What does 'succumb' mean?"

"Drops dead. Let's see it." Arnold inched closer.

The three read it together. *Heart attack. While in kitchen of home.*

"I'll bet," Arnold gasped, "she was putting things in those cupboards."

Husband finds body . . . recently moved here from Bridgeport. Active member of garden club, grew prize-winning roses. Husband with United Electric . . . services will be held . . .

Chip closed the book and laid his hands solemnly on the cover. "That tells us everything. She did die suddenly. And you know what they say about sudden deaths." He looked at the blank faces of his friends. "Peo-

ple who die suddenly or violently often come back to haunt the place they died."

Maury looked depressed. "Does that mean that we're stuck with her for good?"

"Nope. Sometimes the departed just come back to wind up unfinished business. Maybe we can help her along. She died in the kitchen . . ."

". . . Putting things away!" Maury's eyes blazed with excitement. "Maybe that poor ghostly brain wants the pots and pans put away in a special way."

"Hey, you may have something there." Chip turned to Arnold. "What do you think? Arnold, what's wrong?"

Arnold was leaning weakly on the table. "I think I'd better get home. I feel awful."

He wasn't faking. Chip looked at Maury with concern. "Watch him, will you, Maury? I'm going to call my mother. She'll take him home." He laid his hand on Arnold's shoulder. "Take it easy, huh? She'll be right here. I'll watch for her at the door and come and get you."

Mrs. Sanders said she'd be right over. As Chip stood on the library steps waiting, his thoughts drifted from the boys inside to the item they had just read. Something about it, something unexpected, stirred his memory. Something he'd never heard before. *Garden club. Prize-winning roses.* That was it! Flowers! When the ghost had walked in the room that night, and Chip heard the steps and

114

had felt that awful cold, there had been something else. Something that had faded in the excitement. There had been a scent. A very faint scent. It had come into the room with the ghost and disappeared with her. And that scent was the scent of roses!

13

The Success Pattern

ARNOLD HAD a very bad cold. He had to stay home, for days. "I won't be able to go to any more swim classes, either," he told Chip on the phone. "I don't mind that so much, but I sure hate missing school."

"You must be delirious to say a thing like that."

"It means missing fun stuff, this time of year," Arnold explained. "And don't forget I'll have to make up the work. Maybe even during the Christmas holidays."

"It's bad timing," Chip agreed. "On another account, too. The Mrs. Gaynor ghost business. You want to go along when we try to exorcise her, don't you?"

"I sure do." Arnold paused. "How are we going to do it?"

He *would* have to ask. "I don't know," Chip confessed. "I'm doing some deep thinking."

"According to my research," Arnold said, pausing for a sneeze, "there are mean ghosts and helpful ghosts. What category would you say Mrs. Gaynor falls in?"

"Someone said she was feisty and stubborn. Making her husband build a two-story house was one example. But mean? I don't know."

"She doesn't seem to do any actual damage. Do you suppose she is trying to be helpful in some way?"

"I can't see how walking into rooms or barging around in closets could be helpful," Chip said. "Or slamming those kitchen cupboards. Unless"—he got a tighter grip on the phone—"she's trying to tell them something."

"You might have something there."

The boys were silent, exploring this new idea.

"Think about it," Chip said. "If you get any brilliant ideas, give me a buzz."

Arnold buzzed back the next day.

"I dug around in some old books," he said, his voice full of excitement, "and found that paperback of true ghost tales, you know, the one I loaned you one time?"

"Go on . . ."

"There was one story about the woman who found an old picture in the attic of a house she bought. She hung it, but it kept falling off the wall in the middle of the night. Finally, she moved it over the fireplace and from then on, it stayed. She figured the ghost must have wanted it there."

"So?"

"Maybe Maury was onto something the

117

other day when he suggested changing the kitchen equipment around. Maybe Mrs. Gaynor wants the pans put into a different cabinet."

"I'll give Maury a call and tell him to get right on it. Keep thinking, Arnold. We may crack this case before Christmas."

Maury was eager to try the kitchen experiment. "I'll offer to help my mother clean cupboards for the holidays," he said. "She mentioned, the other day, she planned to change things around a little. Maybe that will do it. I'd sure like to get that spook out of the house. Especially my bedroom."

"Has she been back?"

"Has she ever! Practically every night. I keep repeating to myself what you said, that if you want to lick something you have to face it. But frankly, I get paralyzed. Besides, how can you face something you can't ever see, or touch?"

"But that you can hear . . . and *smell!*" Chip had been meaning to compare notes with Maury. "Have you ever noticed a certain scent when the ghost comes into the room?"

"Hmmmmmm. . . ."

"A smell of flowers?"

"Now that you mention it, yes. Faint, though."

"Roses?"

"I'm not that familiar with flowers."

"Well, I am, with roses. I wish ours were still blooming. Anyway, notice the next time she walks, will you? See if you can pick up the scent."

"I sure will. And I'll get going on the cupboards."

"Scent of what?" Fran asked, walking into the kitchen with her kitten just as Chip hung up. "Are you planning on buying a catnip toy for Gypsy for Christmas?"

"I wasn't planning on buying her anything," Chip said. "I'm no Rockefeller, you know. And since when is she *Gypsy?* I thought you were naming her Princess."

"I'm trying out different ones to see which fits. Any suggestions?"

"Marshmallow. You could call her Marsha for short."

"She's black and white," Fran said witheringly. "She doesn't look like a marshmallow."

"Sure she does. A toasted one."

"Oh, sick."

Chip leaned his elbow on the counter and watched Fran pour milk for her pet. It was a pretty cat all right, but it didn't have the personality of Rosebush. *Rose*bush. He straightened. Wasn't it strange that Maury, who knew nothing about flowers, had named his cat after the scent that surrounded the ghost? Chip felt a tingling at the back of his neck. Could this have been a case of psychic suggestion?

He got worse than shivers the next week at swim class. It was closer to cold chills. Mr. Al

Wolf was bearing down on them to master all the Beginner's requirements.

"It's hard to believe," he said at the end of Tuesday's session, "that we've only got four more classes before test day, the seventeenth. Some of you characters aren't even doing an acceptable back float."

Was it Chip's imagination that the instructor's eyes lit on him a shade longer than was strictly necessary?

"On Thursday we're going to work on individual weaknesses. Then we're going to concentrate on test requirements. There's no reason why everyone here can't make the grade. Dismissed."

Lucky Arnold, Chip thought, dragging to the dressing room. Home safely sick in bed, while here he was, doomed to four more miserable classes and then probable failure. His family and friends would wonder, and the kids in class would whisper and laugh behind their hands. Maybe right now he should walk outside without his shoes, through the inch or so of snow, and catch a good cold. Then no one would expect anything of him at all.

It's not fair, he thought. Expecting so much of me. I'm just a little—*coward?* A voice seemed to say. No! He wasn't. He just hadn't—*put out much effort?* Well, what was the use? He couldn't pass the test, and that's all there was to it.

* * *

On Thursday, the boys were sent off alone to practice their biggest weakness. It was a toss-up for Chip. He was weak on everything. In the shallow end of the pool, he tried his best to float, but the minute he felt the water lapping dangerously near his nose he fought to stand up.

"Ever see a cork sink?" a voice said behind him.

Wiping the water from his eyes, Chip turned. Derek Peterson was bobbing up and down in the water. "Corks can't sink," he said. He popped under the water and up. "They come right back to the surface. You won't sink, either."

Chip eyed him.

Derek eyed him back, water running from his hair along the side of his face. "You're a cork. You're going to rest on top of the water and let it hold you up. You are going to float."

Chip eyed him some more. Then, as though hypnotized, he leaned back and let the water support him.

"You can float," Derek repeated. "Just keep that in mind."

Chip kept it in mind. He even thought about it in bed that night. "I can float," he told himself, and his bed became the swimming pool, and he could feel the water gently lapping against his body. His feet seemed to float. His legs and body relaxed. His arms became weightless and his head . . . so pleasant. He let go of his thoughts. The next thing he knew it was morning.

"Remember this," Derek told Chip next session when they were getting ready to jump in and swim across the width of the pool. "It is impossible to fail. You have the ability to swim. Before you jump, imagine yourself doing it well."

Chip nodded. Derek not only wasn't missing any marbles, he might be the brightest guy Chip had ever met. It certainly was a comfort, having him there. Derek's turn came just before Chip's. Chip watched the bigger boy cut cleanly through the water, and he imagined he was the one doing the strokes. When Derek pulled out of the pool onto the opposite side, Chip plunged in.

I'm Derek, he thought. I'm a good swimmer. I'm going to head right for that opposite side, and lift my arms and pull forward and kick. It worked! He knifed across and he was hardly winded.

He got out, pulled the water from his eyes with both hands, blinked, and walked around to rejoin the group. "Nice going, Sanders," the coach remarked. He made a megaphone of his hands. "Kick!" he yelled to the boy splashing his way across.

Chip wanted to thank Derek, but he didn't know what to say. Besides, they were separated for the rest of the session, and in the locker room, the four boys were clowning around as usual, right in the way.

He thought about Derek's ideas a lot, though. They gave him a whole new feeling of power. The success pattern. Wasn't that what Derek had called it? It didn't seem kooky now.

By Thursday he was really geared for success. With Derek near at hand, he practiced rotary breathing and front to back flip. He felt confident that by the next week he'd be ready for the test. Derek, himself, was going great guns. It was hard to imagine he had ever felt unsure of himself.

14

Chip's Own Private Ghost

THAT SATURDAY, Arnold was feeling better, but he was still being kept indoors and couldn't have company. Chip wanted to go to Maury's, but his parents were too busy to drive him. It was too cold to walk all that way.

"You can go with me next Saturday when I run over to help Aunt Margaret set up their tree," Mr. Sanders said. "Why don't you finish up your shopping today? Christmas is less than two weeks away."

"Finish up? I haven't even started."

"Then that makes two of us," Mr. Sanders said with a groan. "Do you know what I have to do today? I have to go into a woman's clothes shop and pick out what your mother calls a hostess gown. 'Something elegant and impractical,' she said. That's what she wants. I'd rather take a beating."

"Dad," Chip said, "it's no use holding back. Just go in there and face it."

"I think I'll ask your Aunt Margaret to do it."

"Are you a coward?"

"Yes."

Chip thought of explaining the success pattern to his father but decided against it. "Could I have an advance on my allowance?"

"Sure." His father pulled three dollars out of his pocket with hardly a glance, handed them to Chip, and dialed Aunt Margaret.

Chip wandered through the variety store. He found a star-shaped pin for his mother and a medallion for Fran with a hippy love-legend on it. He was looking around for ideas for the rest of the relatives when he saw something. Artificial roses, so lifelike you wanted to lean over and sniff them. He did. They were perfumed.

He could almost feel the chill of Mrs. Gaynor's ghost as she walked into the room. She must really have loved roses if she still carried the scent with her. Maybe . . . maybe if Maury put a rose in his room, the ghost would take it as a friendly gesture and go, forever. Or maybe she'd give a sign, a clue as to why she walked through the house at night.

Real roses were expensive. Chip knew from experience: he'd helped buy some for Fran when she was in a play. But these were only a quarter each.

Chip bought one. And while he was keyed up with the idea, he bought a large brown envelope, put the rose inside, and went to the post office and mailed it to Maury. The rose might be the catalytic agent to bring the case to a climax!

Maury seemed dubious when Chip called that night to explain. "What's it supposed to prove?" he asked.

"That it's really the ghost of Mrs. Gaynor, for one thing. Maybe she'll take it as an offering, and scram. I don't know, Maury. I'm just scrabbling around for ideas."

"I'll put the rose on the chair," Maury said. "The chair she always sit on."

"Great. Wait until Friday, will you? So I can see the evidence when I come Saturday?"

"Sure."

Any other week would have seemed endless. This last week before the holidays was crammed with so many things, Chip was in a whirl.

Arnold was back in school, but had to be driven to and from. Chip went over Monday night to help explain some of the back work. He also told Arnold about the ghost plans and promised to use all his influence to get him to Maury's house on Saturday. They were going to explore every inch of the closet and spread ashes on the floor, for starters.

Tuesday was the last swim class before the test. Chip knew now he had nothing to fear.

Wednesday night Chip and his parents went to school to hear the junior high choral concert.

On Thursday, they were so busy in school, making decorations for the party the next day, he thought about the swim test only fleetingly. With Derek there, he knew he could do it.

Only Derek wasn't there. Not in the locker room.

He wasn't out by the pool, either.

"You'll be third in line, Sanders," the coach said. "Peterson's out for today."

Out! "What happened?" Chip stammered.

"Some family problem. He'll make up the test later. Okay, let's get ready. We'll go right down the line."

Chip felt as though strings were tightening around him, cramping his insides. I can't do it, he thought. Not without Derek.

The first boy jumped in and did the face float and then the back float.

I'll pretend I'm sick, Chip thought.

The second boy jumped in.

It isn't fair. I didn't expect to have to do it alone!

"Sanders!"

Chip jumped in. The front float was easy.

"Over now."

Chip flopped over. The water rushed at him. It was going to flow right over him.

You're a cork. Corks float. Derek's words pounded at his ears. Chip relaxed and the tenseness flowed from him. He floated.

"Next."

He felt sick. He really did. But he had started. Maybe he could last.

The next series of tests was not exactly easy, but Chip fought them through. Now came the big one. Swimming the length of the pool. Could he do it? No, he couldn't.

The first boy jumped in and began swimming.

I'll tell the coach I feel bad, Chip said to himself. Some other time, when I feel better—he paused. When? When Derek was there? Did he really need him so much? Chip's eyes were on the pool, but now he was seeing Maury. And hearing Maury's words, "Now, if that isn't cool courage, I don't know what is."

The first boy pulled out of the pool and the second began his swim. It was easy enough to be brave about ghosts, Chip thought. Something you couldn't see. Swimming was different. It was downright dangerous. *But was he really in danger?* With the coach standing by? Or was it all in his mind?

Think success! With knees almost buckling, Chip walked to the edge of the pool. I can do it, he told himself. I'm going to jump in and plow right through—the *whistle!* He jumped.

It is impossible to fail. Yet, he floundered. He had seventy-five feet of water to get through. Too much, too much. He lashed out, but he couldn't make any headway. *Relax. Imagine yourself doing it well.* His muscles relaxed. He reached out for the water and let his kicks help carry him along. *Now you're getting with it. Relax. Breathe.*

But it was such a struggle. He just hadn't prepared himself, those last few minutes before he'd jumped. He had counted on concentrating on Derek, and hypnotizing himself into the same pattern. But now, he was lost.

Kick! Lift the arm, take a breath! Do it the way Derek does it. I'm Derek, he tried to tell himself, but Chip kept getting mixed in it. Breathe, you dope, don't try to fight it.

He was moving more smoothly. His breathing was getting better, and he was synchronizing his movements. Don't forget to kick! If he could just last . . . if he could keep up his energy. Not much farther to go. Don't fight it. Take it easy. A little more . . . a little more . . . there! The edge was close. Just another few feet away. He touched the side. He had made it.

Later, breathing deeply, all muscles trembling, Chip watched the other boys without really seeing them. He had passed the test. And for the first time he could look at the pool calmly. It was only a body of water.

Chip, he thought, you've done it. You've exorcised your own private ghost. From now on he felt he could face anything, if he only had the right attitude. It was a simple case of mind over matter.

15

The Spirit Takes Revenge

ON SATURDAY morning, Chip woke up happy. Christmas vacation had officially started. First thing today, he was going to help pick out their Christmas tree. Then when his dad went to Aunt Clara's to set up her tree, Chip and Arnold were going to ride along as far as Maury's.

Big plans were under way. Maury had called the day before to say he had received the rose. He said he would put it on the rush-bottomed chair for the night. He was also going to strew ashes in the closet.

"Any more cupboard noises since you rearranged them?" Chip had asked.

"No. Except when Rosebush crawls inside to get at his cat-nibble food."

"I see." Chip had to be coldly clinical. "There could have been mice there before," he said. "And now they've left, because of the cat. But really, Rosebush is too young to do them harm."

"The mice wouldn't realize that. One whiff of *cat* and they'd scram."

Chip still believed it was the rearrangement that had quieted things in the kitchen. They were closing in on the ghost of Mrs. Gaynor.

Mr. Sanders came in from the garage where he had been warming the car. "Let's get going."

Chip had been about to call Maury. But it would be more exciting to wait and find out what happened last night at the Gaynor house. Had the ghost walked? Would they see her footprints?

The car tires crunched in the snow as they backed out. "Look, ice in the ditch," Chip said.

"The milk was frozen this morning, too. And the doorbell is out of commission. I'll try to find time to fix it today."

The tree lot was jammed with customers.

"Your mother says she likes the kind with a heavy pine fragrance," Mr. Sanders said. "But I can't smell a thing, with my nose numb. Wonder who's in charge here?"

A man in a red plaid jacket and green stocking cap finally steered them to the balsam firs. They bought a bushy one, which they stowed in the back of the station wagon. Only now they couldn't close the back window.

By the time they finished their other errands, it was noon. Mrs. Sanders had hot soup and sandwiches waiting.

"We're not going to eat!" Chip wailed.

"Don't make a production of it," his mother said, glancing through the mail. "Just get it down."

"I'm in a hurry to get to Maury's," he complained.

"Speaking of Maury"—she paused to slit open an envelope—"he called. Oh, Ed, here's a card from the Humes. Did we send them one?"

"Maury called!" Chip's voice was a shriek. "Why didn't you tell me?"

"I just did. And there's no need to shout. Dare I add that Arnold also called? He'll meet you here, he said." Mrs. Sanders looked out the window. "In fact, here he comes now, bundled up to his eyebrows. I'm glad he's out and about again."

On the way across town, Chip murmured to Arnold with a warning look, "Maury called when I was gone this morning, so I don't know any developments."

Arnold nodded wisely.

When Mr. Sanders let the boys off at Maury's, they waited until his car was down the street before they trudged up the shoveled front walk. The house had a dark, brooding look. Chip felt a heavy coldness deep inside him.

"Come on," he urged. "Let's ring the bell."

There was no answer.

They rang again. They could hear no echoes in the house.

Chip looked at Arnold and saw a reflection

of his own foreboding. "Where is he?" he murmured.

"Knock."

Chip rapped on the doorpost. Nothing. Arnold took off his bulky mitten and began banging on the door itself.

They heard faint sounds from inside the house. They drew back, protectively.

Silence, then the door opened. They pulled away. Maury.

"Oh, it's you." He looked relieved. "I thought I heard sounds, but I didn't realize at first that the doorbell wasn't working."

"No kidding," Chip commented. The boys kicked off their boots and went inside. "Ours isn't either. Frozen, I guess."

"Really?" Maury looked relieved. "So that's why some of the lights—"

"Oh, no." Arnold's voice was muffled as he unwound a furry scarf from his face. "Lights wouldn't be affected, because—"

"Are you alone?" Chip interrupted, glancing around.

"Yes. I thought you'd never get here. My folks went to pick up Alberta. She has a lot of stuff to drag home."

"What happened?" Chip asked. "Last night?"

"Let's go upstairs." Maury's eyes darted about unhappily. "It's so gloomy down here."

They nodded and followed him up the dim, curving stairs.

A light was on at the end of the hall, and in

Maury's room they were ablaze, even though it was still afternoon. He closed the door.

"Well?" Chip urged.

Maury pointed to the chair. The rose was lying undisturbed.

Chip blinked in disappointment. "You sure that's the exact way you laid it there?"

"I'm sure."

Arnold picked up the rose, twirled it and tossed it onto the desk. "So she doesn't like fake flowers." He sat on the squeaky seat and looked up at the ceiling. "Yoo hoo! Mrs. Gaynor! I'm sitting on your chair!" He raised his eyebrows at the boys. "She must be off scribbling a letter to Santa."

Chip turned his back. "How about the ashes? Did you put them out?"

Maury nodded. "Last night."

"And?"

"Nothing. I checked this morning."

Chip sank on the side of the bed in disappointment. "Then it's a failure," he said.

"Oh, I don't know," Arnold said carelessly. "The ghost doesn't walk every night, does she?"

"No, but"—Maury hunched on the bed opposite Chip—"I have this awful feeling she came in . . ." His voice trembled.

"Why?" Arnold leaned forward.

Chip plopped beside Maury and took his arm. "What happened?"

"Rosebush"—Maury's voice broke—"Rosebush is missing."

"Missing!" Chip looked around the room. "Are you sure? Maybe he's outside. Did you let him out?"

"He never wanders away."

"Did you see him last night?" Arnold asked.

"I just can't remember," Maury said. "We went to visit some people my parents know and I was sleepy by the time we got home. The last thing before going to bed, I put out the rose and ashes, but I can't remember . . ."

"Well, didn't you feed him?"

"I don't know," he said with a groan. "Sometimes my mother does, sometimes I do. His dish was empty this morning, and when I put out his food I realized he hadn't been around." He looked at Chip. "Why are you staring at me like that?"

Chip glanced at Arnold and then lowered his eyes. "Why," he asked quietly, "did you name him *Rosebush?*"

"I told you! His claws . . ."

"Think. *Rose*bush. Doesn't it strike you as strange that . . ."

Arnold hunched forward, eyes widened. "Are you suggesting some theory of ESP? Boy!"

"Psychic suggestion," Chip said mysteriously. "Maury, did you sit down with pencil and paper to think up names, or did the word *Rosebush* creep into your conscious mind?"

Maury concentrated. "His claws and bushiness. The name just occurred to me, out of the blue."

Chip and Arnold exchanged significant looks.

Chip shifted his gaze to Maury.

"What did Rosebush do when the ghost walked at night?"

"Nothing. I usually grabbed onto him and held him." He looked from one boy to the other. "What are you getting at?"

Chip bit his lip. "I'm afraid we may have offended Mrs. Gaynor. By offering her that artificial rose."

Maury's eyes were enormous. "Why?"

"She wanted the real thing."

A low sob came from Maury. "But Rosebush is a *cat!*"

"To which," Arnold said intently, "you gave the name of her favorite flower."

Maury's hands clutched the bedspread. *"No!"*

The three of them sat speechless, staring.

"Do you suppose . . ." Arnold began.

"Sssssssh!" Chip's body became rigid. "What was that?"

They sat like frozen bodies, listening.

"What?"

Chip gave a warning shake of his head. They all strained forward.

There were noises downstairs. Footsteps.

"Your folks?" Chip whispered.

Maury gave a violent shake of his head. "Not yet." His lips barely moved.

The steps were on the stairs now. There was no other sound. Just the steady clump, clump,

clump. The other night, Chip thought, it might possibly have been his imagination. But these footsteps today were real. And they were coming nearer!

Arnold slid to the floor between the beds. Maury and Chip scrambled down beside him. They waited. From their crouched position they heard those steps. Closer, closer. Now they were at the top of the stairs.

"Mama . . ." Arnold whispered. Chip gave him a sharp nudge.

Chip's body was stiff with fear, and yet it trembled. He hardly breathed, waiting for the door to open. There was a pause in the sounds. Then a slight clink of metal. He seemed to have stopped breathing.

The footsteps again. But they were going down the hall. Chip let out his breath. In a moment, he raised his head, listening.

The sounds were in Alberta's room now. Yes . . . at the closet. He heard the doors sliding open. The ghost was only a few yards away, beyond the wall.

The boys sat together, arms gripped, listening.

There was a grating sound, and then a noise from higher up.

"The ladder," Maury whispered. "In Berta's closet. The spook is going up the ladder!"

"Ladder?" Arnold asked.

Chip remembered. Yes, he had seen it that first time at Maury's. And it was the thing that had been teasing his memory ever since.

"What is it for?" he whispered. How could he have forgotten the ladder?

"There's a door in the top of her closet," Maury said.

"Leading to what?"

Maury shivered. "I don't know. I steer clear of that closet."

"It must be an attic." Chip's heart was racing. "And there's something up there I bet that Mrs. Gaynor is trying to get at. Maybe a treasure. Maury, we should have . . ."

"Ssssssh . . ."

There were slight scuffling sounds overhead now. Very faint. Something—or someone—was moving around.

"Let's go," Chip said, disentangling himself. "Let's have a look."

"In that room?" Arnold blinked rapidly. "You must be out of your skull!"

"It's now or never," Chip said, stepping over legs. "I'm all for facing up to that ghost." Somehow, his friends' fright gave him courage. "Coming?"

Maury looked at Chip wide eyed. He got to his feet as though in a trance.

Chip started for the door. Maury followed.

"Hey," Arnold hissed. "Don't leave me!" He had that pinched look, as if he was about to sneeze.

Chip slowly opened the door to the hall and paused. The sounds continued overhead. He edged along the wall, down the hall to Alberta's room. That door was open. Again, he paused. Now, there was no place to hide. He turned to see if Maury and Chip were behind him. They were, scary eyed.

Chip took a deep breath and walked softly into the room. Pause. It was quiet up above.

He took another step forward. Another. Now he was before the open closet door. He gasped and pulled back. Then he pointed. The ashes on the closet floor were tracked!

He took a small step forward. Arnold's and Maury's hands were gripping his arms just above the elbows.

He leaned forward to get a closer look. Right next to the ladder the ashes were all trampled. No distinct prints.

There was a small sound overhead. He raised his eyes to the black opening.

It all happened so suddenly . . .

A sound. A fuzzy face with staring eyes at the edge of the gaping blackness. And then a lurch . . . and a small black body came hurtling from above to land with a sickening thud at their feet.

"Rosebush!" Maury screamed. *"He's dead!"*

16

Up There in the Attic

THE BOYS looked with horror at the clump of lifeless fur at their feet.

"He's dead," Maury repeated, sobbing. He fell to his knees.

"Who's dead?" The voice, coming from the opening up above, sent the other boys to their knees.

"Who's dead, I say?" The voice was old and cranky-sounding.

Chip's jaw was working, but no sound came out.

Arnold whimpered softly.

Footsteps overhead now . . . and as the boys watched, panic-stricken, a foot appeared on the ladder.

Arnold moved as though to crawl to the door. Chip got a grip on his ankle and yanked him back.

Another foot appeared. *They were men's work shoes!*

"I'm just visiting here," Arnold quavered.

"Shut up," Chip hissed.

A pair of worn work pants appeared. An old blue flannel shirt. A face leaned down and looked at them. It was only an old man!

"Hi, young fellas," he said. "Wondered who was down here. Live here, eh?"

"I do," Maury said with a quaver.

"Well, maybe you can lend me a hand." He came all the way down and shuffled through the ashes. "Say"—he eyed Rosebush— "what happened to this cat?"

"You killed him," Chip said.

"Killed? Naw." He reached down with his big-knuckled hands and gently shook the cat. "Stunned, I'd say. Must have touched a wire." He rubbed the front paws. "And took a tumble, looks like. Come on, kitty, look alive now."

It was unbelievable. An ear twitched, then a paw.

"Come on now, join the party," the old man urged.

Rosebush blinked, shook his head, and tried to rise.

"Rosebush! You're alive!" Maury scooped up his cat and rubbed his face against the fur. "Oh, Rosebush!"

The old man scratched his head. "That cat must have been up there since yesterday. Guess I forgot about him."

"Yesterday? How?" Chip wanted to know.

"I took him up with me when I came to

check the wiring. Thought there might be a mouse or two up there causing mischief, and so I didn't see any harm in taking the little feller up to nab them while I was working away."

Maury raised his head from the cat. "Working away at what?"

"The light connections, boy. When I called to check up, your daddy said sure you were having trouble with the lights blinking on and off so I figured it might well be the junction box. Sure enough. The lid was off, and some of the wiring exposed. Could have caused you a good deal of trouble. Lucky thing I called. Wouldn't want this house to burn down, now would you?"

"But who are you?" Maury asked. "Why did you call?"

"Why, I'm Joe Gaynor, son. Man who built this house. Least, I did the wiring. That's way back when the Missus, God rest her soul, was alive and kicking."

"But . . ." Chip insisted, "why did you call Maury's dad?"

Mr. Gaynor shook his head. "Darndest thing. I'd been having dreams. Seems the Missus was leading me to this house and up that ladder. But I never quite made it up the ladder. Always woke up." He gave an embarrassed cackle. "Now, I don't set store by such things, but a short time ago I got a phone call, asking questions about this house. About the Missus, too. I just couldn't take my ease after that. Seemed so peculiar . . . those dreams and then that phone call." He scratched behind his ear.

"Then what?" Chip prodded.

"I found out who lived here, and gave a call. Sure enough, things weren't right with the lighting, so I thought best to come over and check her out."

"And that was yesterday?" Maury asked.

"It was yesterday I came over," Mr. Gaynor agreed, "and found there was a part or two needed replacing. So I went out and got them and I'm back today. Now I'd best go up and finish my work. Cat all right now, sonny?"

Maury nodded.

The old man started up the ladder.

"Why didn't you ring the doorbell today . . . oh . . ." Chip stopped. "It wasn't working."

The old man dipped his head in agreement. "One of the wires I left loose yesterday. Knocked today, but nobody answered, so I just walked in. Hope I didn't scare you none." He nodded politely and finished climbing the ladder.

Chip exhaled loudly. "There's your light mystery, Maury. Loose connections, bad wiring, and so on."

"That explains it, all right," Maury said, petting his cat. Rosebush licked him weakly.

From downstairs came a sound of voices and a sudden blare of music.

"They're back with Alberta," Maury said, jumping up.

The music volume increased and broke into ear-shattering sound as Alberta burst into the room with a transistor.

"Hi, you bums," she said gaily, turning down the volume. "What are you doing in my room?"

"Waiting while Mr. Gaynor fixes the lighting up there," Maury said.

"Oh, yes." Alberta switched stations. "Dad said he was coming over."

"He didn't tell me."

"Maybe you didn't ask. What's all that gook on the floor?"

"Ashes."

"Oh." She yawned and flicked off the radio. "Why don't you toads clear out of here now? I want to grab a nap."

Arnold and Chip merely blinked.

"The man's working up there in the attic," Maury said.

"That's okay. I'll turn off all sound."

"I'd sure like to see what's up there," Chip said, peering toward the opening in the closet.

"Be my guest," Alberta said, draping herself in a blanket. "There's nothing there but a lot of junk. Maury, you ought to clear it out some time."

"You've been up above?" Maury was incredulous. "You never told me!"

"You didn't ask." Alberta closed her eyes and flipped a corner of the coverlet over her face.

The boys scurried up the ladder. Sure

enough, Alberta's old ice skates, skis, and other bulky belongings were stacked near the entrance.

Mr. Gaynor looked up from his work. "You ought to tell your folks next time they leave up here to be sure to close that ceiling door all the way. Otherwise, you'll get a cold draft through the whole upstairs."

"What's that, over there in the corner?" Maury asked.

Mr. Gaynor looked over his shoulder. "Some of my wife's belongings. Forgot all about them when I moved." His face took on a melancholy look. "See those bunches of dried flowers hanging on the posts? Mrs. Gaynor's prize roses. She never could let go of things."

The rose scent! And the draft from the attic. No wonder Chip had thought he smelled flowers.

Before Mr. Gaynor left, the boys helped him haul the things he wanted from the attic. Mr. Kinkade met them downstairs.

"Everything all set now?" he asked.

"Far as the electricity is concerned. But it might be best to check out the heating. Seems to me your fan control is a mite off. Blower turns on before the heat takes over. Could be you've noticed a sudden chill?"

Maury gave Chip a quick look.

"I'll have someone in," Mr. Kinkade said. "My wife has mentioned the cold." He glanced at Maury. "There have been sounds, too. Could that be caused by the heating?"

"Why sure. You've got a split system here, you know. Hot water and forced air. I was able to swing it by trading labor with a heating man. Anyway, your duct work in the hot water system could make the floorboards expand and contract. Your forced-air heating will give some irregular sounds, too. Especially when the filters need changing."

"I'll see to it right away," Mr. Kinkade said. He put his hand on Maury's shoulder. "We're very much obliged to you, Mr. Gaynor. More than you realize."

On Christmas afternoon, Maury's folks dropped him off at Chip's. Arnold was there and all three were going to play ice hockey. Veronica and Fran were going to the rink, too, to try out their figure skates.

"Debbie will be here in a few minutes," Fran said. "She says she got a darling new skating outfit for Christmas."

"Let's leave," Chip said.

"Maury," Veronica said, "is the Gaynor case officially closed? Chip was telling me about it."

Maury grinned. "Sure. As you probably know, the so-called ghost was just the elaborate heating system, and a few other things."

"I know what you mean. That first winter we were here, I heard all kinds of strange sounds. I wasn't used to furnace noises."

Fran looked wistful. "Wouldn't it be exciting, though, if it really had been a ghost? A Spook House come to life!"

"I'll bet Maury doesn't think so. Or his mother. The two of them alone in that creepy house."

"We won't be alone so much now," Maury said. "My dad is getting moved to another department, so he'll hardly ever have to travel."

"Speaking of traveling," Veronica said, "here comes Debbie. She looks straight from Siberia with all that fur."

"Let's duck out the back way," Chip said.

The three boys headed for the pond, carrying hockey sticks and skates. They walked single file through a shortcut path, and, when it widened, walked beside each other. The air was crisp, and the snow crunched with each step.

"Even so," Chip finally said, his breath a ghostly vapor, "I could have sworn, that night, I heard footsteps in your room."

"Me, too," Maury agreed. "It shows what imagination can do."

"You haven't heard them since?"

"No."

"That's because," Arnold said, puffing a little, "there never was anything to hear. It was all in your mind."

"We know that," Chip said. "Still if it *had* been the ghost of Mrs. Gaynor, there's a reason why she's quiet now." He paused. "Her work is finished. She's gone to her rest at last, poor soul."

"What work?" Arnold snorted. "All she did was make a disturbance."

"There was a reason," Chip argued. "Her work was to attract the family's attention to that closet, so they'd notice the loose wiring in the attic."

"So she was a friendly ghost after all," Maury said. "Warning us about possible fire."

"Aw," Arnold said, "she was just worried about her old house." He stopped so abruptly his skates banged against his side. Chip and Maury stopped, too.

"Do you realize," Arnold asked, "that we're at it again? Talking ghosts? When we know there's a perfectly rational explanation for everything that happened?" He looked from one boy to the other. "We know that, don't we?"

"Sure," Chip said.

"Sure," Maury said.

Their eyes met and they grinned.

"Last one to the pond is a psychic screwball!" Arnold shouted, racing away.

With a whoop, Chip and Maury tore after him.

ABOUT THE AUTHOR AND ILLUSTRATOR

STELLA PEVSNER began her writing career as a copywriter for a Chicago advertising agency, then moved on as publicity director for a large cosmetics firm. Later she free-lanced until her four children urged her to write children's books.

Ms. Pevsner also wrote *Call Me Heller, That's My Name,* for which she won a Chicago Women in Publishing Award. Her young adult books include *I'll Always Remember You . . . Maybe; And You Give Me a Pain, Elaine,* winner of a Golden Kite Award; and *Cute Is a Four-Letter Word,* which received a Carl Sandburg Award and was selected as a Children's Choice. All of these titles are available as Archway Paperbacks.

Besides writing, the author likes all kinds of arts and crafts and going to large art fairs. She also enjoys ballet and, when she is home from her extensive foreign travels, she is active backstage in the community theater.

Ms. Pevsner lives in Palatine, Illinois, with her husband.

BARBARA SEULING was born and raised in Brooklyn, New York. She was formerly a children's book editor and is now a free-lance writer and illustrator. She has illustrated many books for young people.